Praise for *The Beard*

"Music producer/filmmaker/manager Alan Swyer has finally kept a promise he made long ago to the late, great Ray Charles. The two men became friends while Swyer was producing an album for the soul legend. Ray was fascinated by Swyer's abilities as a storyteller, his many adventures and projects (managing Ike Turner, writing and directing 'The Buddy Holly Story,' making music videos and commercials.) 'You gotta promise me to write a book!' Ray exclaimed. Swyer said yes, but nothing came of it, until, well — now…. It's been described as 'an insider's guide to the cutthroat phoniness of L.A.'s west side nouveau riche.' "

—Liz Smith, *New York Social Diary*

"No writer working today is better at capturing the craven ambition and cut-throat phoniness of LA's West Side nouveau riche. He's a master of this milieu. This time he's created a Gatsby for the dot.com generation! There's no way this won't be a movie!"

—Billy Vera, singer-songwriter of 'At This Moment' and other hits

"Wow. Whatta ride! Alan Swyer has captured the ambition, the energy, the vibe of today's Wannabees in a wildly colorful yarn that rings all too true."

—Lawrence Turman, producer of 'The Graduate'

"The Beard is a comic novel about a working-class Jersey boy trying to find his identity in Los Angeles, even as the world seems to gang up against him. Swyer offers a contemporary reimagining of Billy Wilder's 'The Apartment' that highlights the glitz, folly, and hubris of the tech industry and its giants."

—Steph Cha, author of *Follow Her Home*

"Jersey guy goes to LA, climbs corporate ladder by minding gorgeous mistresses of bosses, but wants true love and meaning. A novel idea."

—Larry Merchant: TV sports commentator/columnist/author

"A wild, fascinating ride all around Los Angeles as Swyer, with a biting satirical touch, lifts the veil on those primarily adept at creating wealth for themselves and the soullessness that ensues. After reading this fast-paced gem of a novel, you may never visit a search engine again without wincing and wondering about the core values of those increasingly in control of the ways in which we communicate."

—Harvey Araton, author of New York Times bestseller *Driving Mr. Yogi*

"Alan Swyer, the eclectic documentarian, has produced not only an entertaining novel, but one that cleverly includes a guide to good food and playlists for great music."

—Ricky Jay, magician, author, actor

"Alan Swyer is one of my favorite contemporary writers, especially when it comes to music and Hollywood. The Beard contains some of one and a lot of the other, with the character and personality to complement both. Writing with the savvy of an insider, he nonetheless also has the sense of humor, irony, and cynicism about Hollywood that connects with Everyman."

—Marian Leighton Levy, co-founder
Rounder Records

"Swyer has woven a mischievous tale with as illuminating and biting a character study as 'The Apprenticeship of Duddy Kravitz'. Deftly told and magnificently structured story with remarkably memorable characters and riotous humor throughout."

—Brin-Jonathan Butler, author of
The Domino Diaries

THE
BEARD

By

Alan Swyer

Harvard Square Editions
New York
2016

The Beard, by Alan Swyer

Copyright © 2016 Alan Swyer

Cover design by Jonas Swyer
None of the material contained
herein may be reproduced or stored
without permission of the author
under International and Pan-
American Copyright Conventions.

ISBN 978-1-941861-12-7
Printed in the United States of
America

Published in the United States by
Harvard Square Editions
www.harvardsquareeditions.org

For Ronni:

De l'aube claire jusqu'a la fin du jour
Je t'aime encore, tu sais, je t'aime.

"Give me chastity and continence, but not yet."
St. Augustine

"It takes a long time to become young."
Pablo Picasso

"The trick is growing up without growing old."
Casey Stengel

Week One

ON A WEDNESDAY morning, having woefully underestimated rush hour traffic in Los Angeles, Calvin Sands quickly gave up his dream of catching a morning glimpse of Santa Monica's fabled beaches. Instead, he was simply praying that somehow, some way, he might manage to show up for the first day of his new internship at the designated time.

Weaving his ancient, not thoroughly reliable, and far from undented VW bug through a dazzling array of luxury cars – Beemers, Lexi, Range Rovers, Porsches, and the occasional Prius, plus every so often a Tesla, Bentley or Maserati – that would have been inconceivable on his home turf of Elizabeth, New Jersey, Calvin couldn't help but feel like the only person in what was known locally as the Westside who was traveling without the benefit of air conditioning, Bluetooth, or a sense of belonging.

With a fear that in addition to being late, he had also somehow managed to get lost, what little was left of his excitement and anticipation was rapidly giving way to not-so-quiet desperation when Calvin suddenly slowed down – eliciting honks galore – then, with a dose of Garden State audacity, swung the VW into a questionable U-turn.

Spotting that rarest of sights on a major SoCal thoroughfare – a pedestrian who didn't look like a tourist or a homeless person – Calvin turned off the vintage Slim Harpo track he was listening to and engendered another chorus of honks by cutting across three lanes, then pulled to a halt in a No Stopping Zone so as to address the well-dressed guy in his mid-twenties who, after kicking a rock, seemed to be wandering aimlessly.

"Any clue how I find 11201 Olympic?" Calvin asked.

Rousted from a mood that looked to be equal parts anger and self-pity, the pedestrian eyed Calvin for a moment as though sizing him up. "Gadzooks?" he finally asked.

Calvin nodded proudly in response, which precipitated first a frown, then a gesture toward a monolithic, seemingly soulless building.

"Lots of luck," was what Calvin was told with what was clearly more than a measure of bitterness.

Inside an eighth-floor orientation room decorated with a style that was often termed, by both fans and detractors, Neo-Jetsons, a stern but attractive woman nearing forty whose name, Beverly Steele, led to her being called (though never to her face) *The Steel Maiden*, glanced at a clipboard, then strode toward the podium at the far end.

Imperiously, she faced the eleven still anonymous young people – seven men, four women – who were waiting anxiously for the business at hand to get under way.

"If I may –" Beverly began, only to stop when suddenly the door flew open, and in burst Calvin. Toting a tattered Howlin' Wolf backpack, and wearing an anomalous outfit of denim shirt and cargo pants, he instantly became self-conscious as he glanced around at those who were supposed to be his peers. Almost all of them, though in different ways, seemed to radiate wealth, worldliness, and sophistication – a few dressed in the latest from GQ or Vogue, some in *haute* preppy, others in boho chic complete with tattoos and piercings.

"And you are?" Beverly Steele asked none too happily.

"C-Calvin Sands."

Beverly studied Calvin momentarily, then gestured for him to take a seat amidst the others.

Calvin tried to maneuver his way inconspicuously into the second row. But with all eyes upon him, he nervously lost his footing and tripped over a blond patrician who would have looked completely at home in a Ralph Lauren ad.

"Sorry," Calvin whispered, only to receive a look of total disdain.

Settling into a seat at last, Calvin fixed his attention on

Beverly Steele, who deftly underscored her dismay by allowing a moment to pass.

"Ladies and gentlemen," Beverly stated with what seemed to be irony once she resumed, "look to your left."

Everyone immediately did as told.

"Now look to your right."

Again the entire group swiftly obeyed.

"One of you will not be here six or seven weeks from now."

Receiving the collective sigh she expected, plus a cringe from Calvin, Beverly smiled.

"Think that's bad? Then please be assured that a few more of you will be let go – or, perhaps wisely, choose of your own volition to leave – in the days and weeks after that."

Instead of a sigh, a collective groan filled the room, together with a wince from Calvin.

"You've heard," Beverly Steele went on, "about the Darwinian concept known as survival of the fittest. Well, for interns here, it's survival not just of the fittest, but also of the smartest. And hungriest. And most determined. Are you catching my drift?"

With no great zeal, the members of the group all nodded.

"I can't hear you," Beverly exclaimed.

"Yes," the entire group mustered unhappily.

"But the good news?" Beverly added. "For those of you who make it across the finish line, the sky's the fucking limit!"

Somehow those words did not entirely manage to fill the room with glee.

"So welcome to Gadzooks," Beverly announced. "And if you've still got an appetite, there's coffee next door in the conference room, plus bagels, Pepto Bismol, and Tums."

As the others, still reeling from the unwelcoming welcoming speech, staggered out, Calvin hesitantly approached Beverly Steele.

"Sorry I was late," he said softly

"You should be."

"Mind if I ask a question?"

"About?"

"Where to live."

"What am I, Craigslist?"

Seeing Calvin flinch, then start to fiddle with his hands, Beverly looked for a moment as though she was about to soften. "Nervous?"

"Should I be?"

"Only if you're a sentient creature," she said, showing little mercy. "Let me explain to you what survival of the fittest means. No help. No postings. No bullshit about *Getting Acclimated* on our website. And no category called *Roommates Needed*. Get it?"

Calvin bit his lower lip for a moment, then nodded.

"But just so you know, there is a *but*."

"Okay –"

"If I can make it –"

"Yeah?"

"Maybe so can you."

"Think so?"

"It depends."

"On?"

"How badly you want it," Beverly said.

Without another word, she turned and walked out the door.

Stepping into the conference room after catching his breath, Calvin couldn't help but get the impression that he had somehow crashed the wrong party.

Squeezing his way toward the food, he made an effort to smile at those who were sipping coffee and nibbling on bagels, but to no avail. With cliques clearly having already formed, he found himself with a sense of being extraneous almost to the point of invisibility. Or worse, a pariah.

Far from thrilled, Calvin grabbed a bagel with poppy seeds, then started to resign himself to being alone when he spotted a shy Latina who, like him, was obviously being ostracized.

"I'm Calvin," he said by way of introduction.

"Violeta."

"Where you from?"

"El Salvador via Pomona College."

Using his partially gnawed bagel, Calvin gestured toward those who were ostensibly their peers. "Nothing like being made to feel welcome."

"We're already the top two candidates."

"In what?"

"The pool that's started."

"What kind of pool?"

"To see who's the first one bounced."

"No shit?"

Violeta shook her head.

"You pissed?" Calvin asked.

"Maybe I'll have tokenism on my side with no other Latinas around," answered Violeta with a shrug. "How about you?"

"I don't know whether to be pissed, motivated —"

"Or?" Violeta asked when Calvin hesitated.

"Turn into a psycho-killer."

"You don't look much like a psycho-killer."

"Just psycho, huh?"

"Well —" said Violeta

"But I'm working on the killer part," Calvin joked as into the conference room stepped a spiky-haired guy not yet thirty who was clearly proud of what he took to be his own importance.

Banging his fist on a table to get attention, the newcomer waited until everyone was looking at him. "Time's a-wasting, boys and girls," he then said haughtily.

With the spiky-haired guy leading the way, the interns returned to the orientation room, where a handsome, blond, athletic man who looked like he could still be the captain of the Yale crew team stood beside Beverly Steele.

"My name, so that you're in the know, is Matt Donnelly," the guy who would soon become known amongst the interns as Mr. Spiky announced once everyone was seated. "You've already had a chance to meet the estimable and formidable Beverly Steele. And this, for those who didn't interview with him, is our distinguished head of marketing, my friend and accomplice in crime Brad Tucker."

Tucker took a step forward, then gazed at the group in front of him. "Lots of companies like to claim that they're cutting edge. Right?"

As one, the interns nodded.

"You call that an answer?" Matt Donnelly piped in.

"Yes," said the interns.

"So fucking nineties," Tucker stated. "We at Gadzooks don't have to bill ourselves as hip, edgy, or any of that cornball shit. We just go about our business, leaving our would-be competitors –"

"– The sinister places we love to refer to as Yoo-Hoo and Goo-Goo," Donnelly interjected.

"– Far behind as we create, adapt, and personalize internet and smart phone technology in never-before-dreamed of ways." The epitome of smugness, Tucker turned to Matt Donnelly. "Am I right?"

"Fuckin'-A!" Donnelly affirmed.

"Not that it'll matter for the ones who don't make the cut," Tucker continued. "But as I point to you, please tell us your name, where you're from –"

"And any pertinent detail," Donnelly added.

Tucker pointed to a thin guy in a Versace suit.

"Imran Habib, from Pakistan, where I was on the national polo team," came the response, which confirmed to Calvin the loftiness of his competition. "Then Stanford, with a junior year at the London School of Economics."

Next Tucker pointed to a very cute Asian woman whose hair was dyed bright red.

"Amy Kawasaki – B.A. Summa Cum Laude with a major in physics and a minor in cinema at Berkeley, followed by post-grad work in marketing en route to an MBA there. Oh yes, I'm originally from Tokyo, which is why I'm bilingual – trilingual if you add pretty good Italian – then Rancho Santa Fe."

Calvin's heart sunk even deeper, then he watched Tucker point toward a fastidiously foppish guy, who promptly smiled as he prepared to speak.

"Robert Williams, Newport, Rhode Island – Bogota, where Dad was Ambassador – then Williams College, which, contrary to popular belief, despite a tradition that's lasted for generations, was not actually named for us. Oh, and Phi Beta Kappa, as well as having had pieces published in both the *New Yorker* and the *Atlantic*."

Feeling more and more nauseous with each passing moment, Calvin turned toward Violeta and whispered. "Got a knife?" he whispered.

"If I did, I'd be using it on myself."

"Then how about cyanide?"

Tucker, meanwhile, pointed toward a tall woman who may well have been both wardrobed and accessorized by Rachel Zoe.

"Samantha Steinberg, Great Neck, B.A. Tisch School at NYU, MBA Wharton – ex-cheerleader, varsity tennis, and president of Model U.N."

Next Tucker turned toward a rugged specimen in a torn Bob Marley t-shirt and a motorcycle jacket.

"Bruce Springsteen, Asbury Park, New Jersey," was the response.

Everyone – Calvin included – shared a much needed laugh, then the speaker continued.

"Actually, Harlan Brooks, III – Harley, to my friends, as in the bike I ride – Darien, Cape Cod, a couple of jail cells, then Dartmouth."

Then, after scanning the interns who had not yet spoken, it was toward the blond patrician over whom Calvin tripped earlier that Tucker pointed.

"Jonathan Olson," he stood up and said with great forcefulness and pride. "Houston raised, Princeton educated, captain of the lacrosse team, then Oxford. Oh, and my father's in *Who's-Who*."

Having by then reached his breaking point, Calvin grimaced when Tucker leveled a finger in his direction, then uncharacteristically threw caution to the wind.

"Calvin Sands from the wrong side of the tracks in what is decidedly not a garden spot in the Garden State: Elizabeth, New Jersey. Then Rutgers on the prestigious five-year work-study, drive-a-delivery-truck-during-the-summer plan. And having spurned *Who's-Who*, my dad opted for the distinguished group known as *So-What*."

For a moment there was not a sound to be heard anywhere, while Violeta gaped but others averted their eyes.

Only when irrepressible Harley Brooks let out a guffaw was the strained silence finally broken. Then Brad Tucker found himself faced with the unpleasant task of focusing on the remaining interns.

Twenty minutes later, like a mother hen leading her chicks, Beverly Steele headed down the hallway as she gave the interns a tour of the Gadzook offices.

"This is the tech command post, the brain center where our search engines are constantly updated," she said as she pointed out a gleaming facility in which an array of scientists, engineers, and geeks labored in an environment that also featured nerf balls, strange posters, and assorted snacks and toys. "This is the spot in which new apps are conceived, exciting technologies are dreamed up, and conventional behavior or thinking – having been banished by royal proclamation – rarely dares to make an appearance."

After allowing her flock to take a lengthy gander, Beverly was about to lead on when toward her came a guy who looked like an aging surfer, complete with a tan, a three-day growth, unkempt hair starting to turn gray, shaggy torn jeans, and flip-flops.

"This," Beverly said as she gestured toward the self-satisfied figure who was bopping in their direction, "is the one and only Steve Norris, Head of Product Development, which in Gadzooks-speak means, among other things, that he's the

King of Apps."

Norris glanced at the interns, paying particular attention to the females, then gave a half-bow. "Welcome one and all," he said theatrically.

"For now," Beverly added.

"Hey," said Norris, "like they say about every bodacious wave in surfing, dig each and every moment while you can."

Vividly aware of the kind of impression he made, Norris smiled, then headed onward.

Shepherding her charges in the opposite direction, Beverly stopped a moment later to point out yet another key spot.

"Here we have the mail room," she announced. "Which will likely be as far as some of you ever progress."

Not surprisingly, those words elicited a gulp from several members of the group. But before resuming her expedition, Beverly suddenly noticed someone else who seemed even more incongruous than Norris, and not only because of his dreadlocks, his faded 76ers t-shirt, his blue warm-up pants, and his vintage Air Jordans.

"This," Beverly said, referring to the black guy of thirty who was approaching, "is the man I call our secret weapon, Alonzo Stevens. Everything good, Alonzo?"

"If everything were really good, nobody would need me around here," Alonzo replied.

"Alonzo," Beverly explained to the interns, "is the guy that I and other knowledgeable people around here turn to when all our IT geniuses from Cal Tech and MIT can't find a way to make things work. Right, Alonzo?"

"If you say so."

The interns eyed Alonzo silently – all, that is, but Jonathan Olson, who grandly stepped toward him.

"What it is, my brother?" Jonathan said, extending a fist so as to fist-bump with Alonzo. But to the delight of Calvin, Alonzo seemed not the least bit pleased and therefore failed to reciprocate.

"Since when are we brothers?" Alonzo asked with explicit disgust.

The other interns – Calvin foremost among them – watched intently as Alonzo, having spurned what he took to be Jonathan's patronizing gesture, continued his journey down the hall.

Lunchtime. As out from the building stepped several of the interns, Calvin, ever hopeful, addressed those in closest proximity to him: Imran, Robert, and Samantha.

"You guys want to grab a bite?"

Looks were exchanged, then Robert spoke. "We've... uhh... got plans?"

Undaunted, Calvin turned to another guy: Jonathan.

"Want to grab a sandwich?"

"I'm not available for that," Jonathan answered with what sounded like undisguised condescension.

Clearly rejected, Calvin looked around and realized that there was only one other intern left nearby: Violeta.

"Buy you a salad or a something?" he asked.

Violeta pulled a brown paper bag out of her purse.

"I brought an empanada. Want half?"

"That's okay, but thanks."

As Violeta wandered off, Calvin couldn't help but feel alone – incredibly alone – both literally and figuratively.

He took a deep breath as though contemplating his fate, then wandered toward the side of the Gadzooks building, where he noticed a sign for a ground-floor breakfast-and-lunch type place called *Cash & Carrie*.

Spotless yet inviting, adorned with photos of various sites in China – the Great Wall, Tiananmen Square, the Yungang Buddhist Grottoes, and the Muslim Quarter in Xi'an among others – plus a blackboard listing several Chinese specials along with standard gringo salads, sandwiches, smoothies, and wraps, the joint was jumping when Calvin stepped in.

Catching sight of the young Asian woman at the Order Counter, who was striking in a surprisingly artsy, bohemian kind of way that seemed at the same time both incongruous yet somehow appropriate, Calvin stopped and stared.

And he was still staring when spiky-haired Matt Donnelly, who was about to leave with a take-out order, spotted him.

"Hot, huh?" Donnelly asked, gesturing toward the attractive young woman.

"Yeah."

"Conrad, right?"

"Calvin."

"Now you know why there's a pool."

"To see who's the first intern bounced?"

Donnelly shook his head. "To be the first to get into her pants."

With a shit-eating grin, Donnelly patted Calvin on the shoulder, then headed for the door. Calvin frowned as he watched him go, then bucked the crowd so as to approach the counter.

There, he stood and stared silently at the pretty woman, whose name tag identified her as the eponymous *Carrie* – until, that is, she playfully broke his reverie.

"Planning on ordering?" she asked. "Or should I just charge you rent?"

"What's good?"

"Well, we've got fish lips... Squirrel snouts... Eel elbows..."

Calvin grinned. Then an older Chinese woman, whose name tag said *May*, leaned toward him.

"Like Asian food?"

"I guess."

"Try the Hainanese chicken," Carrie suggested.

Having strolled alone through the side streets south of Olympic Boulevard while chomping on his take-out lunch, Calvin wolfed the last forkfuls of rice, then tossed the empty container into a nearby dumpster.

Coming upon a small park, he wandered in, then noticed a familiar figure shooting hoops solo: Alonzo Stevens.

Calvin watched for a couple of moments, then approached only when the basketball, having gotten away from Alonzo, rolled toward him.

"Want some company?" Calvin asked as he retrieved the ball and tossed it toward Alonzo.

"Not especially."

"And here I thought maybe you'd be different."

"Then who?"

"My wonderfully welcoming fellow interns."

"Even if I am, that doesn't mean I want company."

Calvin stiffened momentarily, then turned to go, only to be surprised by a voice.

"Yo!" Alonzo yelled.

Calvin faced him.

"Nothing personal," Alonzo explained. "Eight hours a day – five days a week – I've got to put up with people with whom I've got zippity-doo-dah in common. The last thing I want during my little bit of free time at lunch is more of the same."

Disappointed, Calvin scrutinized Alonzo for a couple of moments. Then, without another word, he turned and trudged back for what he figured would be an afternoon of misery.

For Calvin, who was unhappily ensconced in the cheapest East Hollywood motel he could find, a dinner of tacos from a stand frequented by Mexican laborers led to a night of soul searching, punctuated by the sounds of shots being fired; explosions here and there of hip-hop, salsa, and mariachi music; plus a medley of sirens from police cars, fire engines, and ambulances.

Then there was the additional pleasure of periodic buzzing by helicopters overhead.

That he would be alone in California for a few days until his initiation at Gadzooks began had always been a given for Calvin, one he was able to live with and accept. But that he felt far more alone after the first day of an internship which had initially seemed like a dream come true, and for which he had made the solo drive cross-country, was infinitely worse.

Unable to sleep with all that was going on both externally and internally, Calvin resorted to an old trick of his: making lists. First up, as a longtime music fan who had spent countless hours on Youtube and was known to hit thrift shops and swap meets in search of old vinyl, came an attempt to pinpoint his all-time top ten favorite artists or groups. Ray Charles was a certainty, as was Lou Reed, whether alone or with the Velvet Underground. Solomon Burke was also a sure thing. So, too, was Nina Simone. The Stones were considered briefly, then dropped because their later work ranged, in his estimation, from imitative to lame. Cyndi Lauper might well have made the cut if the rest of her work had been anywhere near as memorable as "Time After Time," or as effervescent as "Girls Just Want To Have Fun." Southside Johnny, as someone truer to Calvin's native New Jersey than Springsteen, was a strong contender. So, too, was Thelonious Monk, who hit more responsive chords for him than greats like Coltrane or Miles. And Willy DeVille, whether alone or as part of Mink DeVille. Close, but not quite close enough, were people like Irma Thomas, whose "I Wish Someone Would Care" Calvin revered, and Fontella Bass, singer of the unforgettable "Rescue Me." Then there was what he termed the esoterica: Bobby "Blue" Bland, whose "Two Steps From The Blues" album stood out from the rest of his work; Slim Harpo, whose output of swamp music was small but tasty; and New Orleans legends like Professor Longhair, Benny Spellman, and Ernie K-Doe.

Calvin understood full well that preferring King Sunny Ade, Little Walter, and Jacques Brel to Tupac, Jay-Z, and Beyonce set him apart from most of his contemporaries, as did his lack of interest in Taylor Swift and his total dismissal of Justin Beiber. But unlike his outsider status at Gadzooks, distancing himself from those he considered musically challenged was willful, deliberate, and of his own volition.

In a strange way it made him feel special, a member of the cognoscenti, someone who knew that the Stones' "You Better Move On" was a so-so cover of Arthur Alexander, and that Janis Joplin's "Get It While You Can" was recorded first, and better, by the great Howard Tate.

In the same way, it was a source of pride to think of

Beatles fans as musical dilettantes, people who were too myopic – or perhaps too racist – to appreciate acts like Little Richard or the Isley Brothers, whom the Brits initially aspired to be.

Though Calvin never quite decided on a definitive top ten that night, the exercise was nevertheless a success, since it inevitably tired him out sufficiently so that he was ultimately able to get a couple of hours sleep.

Having learned the hard way about rush hour traffic, Calvin headed west the next morning with far more time to spare, but with significantly diminished enthusiasm.

Questions that had periodically gnawed at him for years – *Who am I? What am I? What in hell am I supposed do with my life?* – ricocheted through his mind as he attempted to gird himself for more embarrassment, more disappointment, and in all likelihood more isolation.

Stunned even more than before by the solipsism of Los Angeles drivers, all of whom seemed to be yakking away on Bluetooth while acting as though signaling before changing lanes would be too high a price to pay, Calvin did his best to practice forbearance. That, despite the fact that for people like him from New Jersey, *forbearance* was no more a part of the everyday vocabulary than *beatitude, serenity,* or *bliss.*

The result was that even with repeated attempts to focus on his breath and think happy thoughts, Calvin was nonetheless boiling as, while listening to James Carr singing "At The Dark End Of The Street," he again made a questionable U-turn, then followed an Audi convertible into the Gadzooks garage.

Down a ramp went Calvin's rickety Volkswagon, which pulled into a space just as a silver Prius headed into the spot beside it.

Out from the hybrid stepped Beverly Steele, who surprised Calvin by acknowledging him with what seemed almost to be a smile.

"Find an apartment?" she asked.

"And give up the wonderful smell of gunpowder in the morning?"

"That bad?"

"It could be worse."

"You mean like Baghdad? Or Nairobi?"

Both of them started to chuckle, then turned to watch a slew of expensive vehicles pass: a Porsche driven by Imran Habib... a Mercedes driven by Robert Williams... a Harley ridden by Harley Brooks... a Lexus with Amy Kawasaki at the wheel.

"Like what you're up against?" Beverly asked.

"I don't even know what to call 'em."

"The sons and daughters of privilege."

Then up came a shiny red Corvette manned by haughty Jonathan Olson.

"So what do you call him?" Calvin wondered aloud.

"Mr. Oil Spill."

Calvin responded with what Beverly took to be a what's-that-mean expression.

"Guess whose daddy is Senior VP at Occidental Petroleum," she explained.

As Calvin acknowledged the comment, into view came a beautifully restored vintage turquoise-and-white Bel Air convertible with a dapper guy in his forties at the wheel.

"Who is that?" asked Calvin, clearly impressed.

"Our Supreme Master."

"Wesley Phillips drives a '57 Chevy?"

"And a '64 ½ Mustang. And a 1960 Bentley. And whatever else he happens to want. Know much about him?"

"Doesn't everyone?" asked Calvin. "In the technology world, he's both a pioneer and an icon."

"And you're impressed?"

"Aren't you?"

"Oh, absolutely," Beverly stated.

Yet somehow Calvin had the sense that her words did not quite ring entirely true.

A few minutes later, Violeta was walking through the halls of Gadzooks engulfed in gloom when Calvin entered.

"You're in luck," she said wearily.

"In what way?"

"You got the mail room."

"That's good?"

"Yours truly's in Siberia."

"Give me that in English."

"The Media Room, where there's nothing but fifteen TV screens and me."

"Which may not be so bad," Calvin said.

"How so?"

"Not likely to be the first place they look when they're searching for someone to cut."

As Calvin's point hit home, Violeta brightened somewhat.

"Think so?" she asked.

"What do I know?" he answered.

Far from thrilled to be stationed in the Mail Room, several of the seemingly anointed interns were sorting through piles of letters, trade papers, and magazines in a desultory way when Samantha Steinberg turned to the guy closest to her, a Filipino from Cal Tech named Rolando Dango.

"So what's your take on Tucker?" she asked.

"To me, he's a big dick," Rolando replied.

From across the room, where he'd been silently going through a pile of of mail on his own, Robert Williams suddenly expressed interest.

"Who's got a big dick?" Robert asked.

Before anyone could answer, into the room stepped Calvin.

The others took notice of him briefly, without uttering a peep, then went right back to what they were doing.

"Guess I'm the invisible man," Calvin announced. "Any of you interested in getting up a softball game this Saturday?"

No answer was forthcoming, so Calvin, determined not to

be daunted, walked over toward Robert.

"Bob, right?" Calvin asked.

"Robert."

"Feel like playing?"

"Please tell me you're joking."

Calvin shrugged, then turned toward Samantha and Rolando.

"How about you two?" he inquired. "Softball? Volleyball? Skinny-dipping?"

"I'll be sailing," Rolando said coldly.

"And I'm flying up to San Francisco," Samantha responded.

Those words, however, were enough to arouse Robert's interest again.

"Want company?" he asked.

Cash & Carrie was once more jumping at lunchtime when spiky-haired Matt Donnelly, with a bag of take-out food in hand, started making his way from the counter.

As he neared the door, in stepped Calvin.

"What up, Conrad?" Donnelly asked.

"Calvin."

Paying no heed to Calvin's correction, Donnelly marched through the door. Calvin watched him disappear, then waved at May while approaching Carrie.

"Another big lunch date today?" Carrie asked once Calvin made his way to the front of the line.

"Angelina Jolie was busy."

"Probably with Brad Pitt, which explains why he's not here with me. Sure you're with Gadzooks?"

"Why?"

"You don't seem like the rest of them."

"Is that good or bad?"

"A place that has pools about who gets into my pants?"

"You know about that?"

"Think discretion's prized anywhere near as much as ambition?" she asked. "So tell me, is your visit here about chatter, or is there maybe a chance you're hungry?"

"And if I say both?"

"I'll take that as corny but flattering," Carrie said. "But I'll also have to start charging you if you don't order something. So tell me, by the minute or by the ounce?"

"So what's healthy but tasty?"

"Ma Po Tofu, which you can have with or without ground pork," Amy answered. "If, that is, you're feeling adventurous."

Ten minutes later, with a large bag of take-out food in hand, Calvin ambled into the small park where Alonzo was back shooting baskets.

"Hungry?" Calvin yelled as he approached.

"My girlfriend usually brings me lunch."

"Want to bet you don't have your cell phone?"

"What's that supposed to mean?"

"She called the office to say she couldn't make it."

Alonzo shrugged.

"Just so happens I'm a vegan," he said.

"Which is why I brought you a Chinese tofu dish that smells great."

"You're relentless," Alonzo said, shaking his head.

"You ain't seen nothin' yet."

Together the two of them strolled toward a picnic table, where Calvin took out the food, then napkins and chopsticks.

"Don't go thinkin' this makes us friends," Alonzo said as he took a seat.

"I wouldn't dare."

"And if I tell you you're full of shit?"

"You wouldn't be the first."

Alonzo gazed at Calvin for what felt like an eternity.

"What makes you think the two of us got something in common?" he finally asked.

"Over at Gadzooks –"

"Yeah?"

"Seems to me we're both outsiders," Calvin stated.

Instead of agreeing or disagreeing, Alonzo simply dug into

the food.

With lunch ancient history, after walking a couple of blocks in silence while dribbling the basketball, Alonzo finally spoke as he and Calvin approached the Gadzooks building.

"So the other interns, they're treating you like shit?"

"Watch for a while, then you be the judge," Calvin replied as the two of them neared the main entrance.

Inside the main lobby, up from the garage rose an elevator, which came to a stop. The door opened, revealing Jonathan Olson, who feigned disinterest at the sight of Calvin and Alonzo as they entered.

"Want to grab a beer after work?" Calvin asked Jonathan as the door closed and the three of them started their ascent.

"I'm not available for that," Jonathan answered condescendingly, drawing what seemed to him to be a perplexing chortle from Alonzo.

Reaching the eighth floor, the elevator door opened again, then out stepped a still somewhat confused Jonathan.

Calvin and Alonzo watched him head down the hallway before emerging.

"Lunch again on Monday?" Calvin asked.

"You know," Alonzo replied, "I may just be available for that."

No longer feeling quite so totally alone, Calvin smiled.

"Thanks, Alonzo."

"My friends call me 'Zo," Alonzo replied, patting Calvin on the shoulder.

Whatever glow Calvin temporarily felt after his time with Alonzo had long since dissipated by that evening, which found him, after another taco dinner, very much by his lonesome in a place he'd come to think of as Motel Hell.

Worse, he had a whole weekend ahead, with no plans, no kinships, and no expectations.

Back home on a Friday night, even one in which he found himself without a date, several choices would have been available. He could go out for pizza or a movie with some buddies. Or play 9-ball at the nearby pool hall. Or watch sports on the multiple TVs at his favorite dive bar while nursing a beer or two.

And on Saturday, he could get into a pick-up basketball game at either the outdoor court at Warinanco Park or the indoor court at the Y, depending on the weather. Or, on a nice day, find a softball game or go for a run.

The truth was that the allure owed less to any given activity than to the simple fact of companionship. The best example of that, Calvin always felt, was a karaoke bar. To be in a place where everyone was having fun, thanks to "Feelings" or "Piano Man" would be an absolute nightmare if alone. But to be in such a place with a friend, or even better a date, would allow for the kind of surreptitious elbowing and laughs that would make the experience fun.

Not that Calvin wanted to romanticize a world from which he had long hoped to escape. From the time he was a kid, he had witnessed what happened to high school heroes whose luster faded more and more with every year that passed. Guys he had looked up to, who at one point had seemed almost larger than life, became sad fixtures at the annual Thanksgiving Day high school football game or at the yearly County basketball tournament, beaten down by dead-end jobs that became a life sentence – if, that is, they weren't at some point laid off.

That's what prompted Calvin to apply for the internship at Gadzooks. And it's what made him want to persist despite the grim and unexpected reality he encountered there.

Unhappy, Calvin flirted with the notion of hitting a bar so as to try one of the Mexican beers he'd heard so much about. But given that the neighborhood was dangerous, and that his available funds were limited, instead he wracked his brain in search of ways to improve what seemed like a stacked deck at Gadzooks.

Unable to come up with suitable answers, Calvin finally climbed into bed. He tossed and turned for what felt like an eternity, then shifted his concentration into another round of list-making.

His first impulse was to focus on the ten best sexual relationships of his life. But that ended quickly when it became clear that even including mediocre experiences, he might still fall short of double digits. So instead Calvin started thinking of books that mattered.

His knee jerk reaction was to think in terms of all-time favorites. But then he reconsidered and decided to include only novels that he'd read since his college days were over.

Jennifer Egan's "A Visit From The Goon Squad" came immediately to mind. So, too, did Junot Diaz's "The Brief Wondrous Life Of Oscar Wao." Then there was the baseball novel that was about far more than baseball, "The Art Of Fielding" by Chad something-or-other whose last name he could never remember. And a couple of great collections of short stories: "Birds Of America" by Lorrie Moore, and "Bad Behavior" by Mary Gaitskill. The list would contain nothing by David Foster Wallace, Calvin decided, since his work, though interesting, never quite hit a responsive chord. And while he was sorely tempted to include Art Spiegelman's "Maus," he refused to nominate "Ender's Game" because of what he considered to be the author's abominable politics. Or Raymond Carver, though the reason for his exclusion might be somewhat unfair, since it was largely a reflection on all those who mimicked the signature style, whether consciously or otherwise. As for John Irving, Calvin often referred to himself as the President of the Garp Resistance League. But though he was lukewarm at best about the Pynchon novels that followed "Gravity's Rainbow," he considered it, like Nabokov's "Lolita," not merely great, but also hysterically funny.

And then Calvin finally drifted off into slumber.

A few hours of fitful sleep, unfortunately, did not make for a joyful Saturday morning. In the hope of fighting his ever-mounting frustration, Calvin went on the internet in search of a picturesque place to run, then put on his gear and drove to Griffith Park.

Jogging in a rustic setting rather than on city streets had a positive effect on both his body and his mind, so after a shower he again turned to Google in search of a place to eat lunch.

The best solution regarding budget, abundance, and adventure seemed to be an Ethiopian restaurant with an all-you-can-eat buffet, which proved to be a pleasant surprise in more ways than one. Even though he pondered playfully if one of the dishes was fried missionary, the food was new to him, and tasty in an exotic way. Plus, instead of feeling geeky eating alone, Calvin found himself surrounded not just by couples and/or families, but also by solitary eaters, some with newspapers, magazines, or iPads, others simply using their fingers to wolf mounds of chicken, lentils, and strange greens thanks to a spongy, crepe-like bread called injera.

What Calvin had often termed postprandial narcosis, especially in the aftermath of a 3 ½ mile run, led to a nap, which took care of much of the afternoon. But then, inevitably, came the night.

Not wanting to give up without some semblance of a fight, Calvin started fiddling with his iPad. His search was for places to go where he would not feel even more alone – like at a Starbucks, for instance, or at a bar where he was certain to know no one – but where he would not necessarily be called upon to spend more of his rapidly dwindling supply of cash. Then to his surprise, his cell phone rang.

Instantly recognizing the caller ID, he answered the same way he'd done many times before.

"Aren't I a lucky guy?" he asked sarcastically.

"Bet your sweet ass!" said his childhood friend Plotkin via Bluetooth as, together with another member of what until recently had been the *three amigos* of a working class neighborhood in New Jersey, he cruised down the Broad Street of their youth in his ratty old Volvo station wagon.

"So when are you coming back to where you belong?" asked the other guy, Ralphie, who as always was stoned out of his gourd.

"And where exactly do I belong?"

"The garden spot of the Garden State," said Plotkin, who was proudly wearing an aging La Bamba & The Hubcaps T-shirt.

"Better known as Dreamland," added Ralphie.

"Dreamland, my ass!"

"C'mon," said Plotkin. "Admit that you miss us."

"Driving around in search of girls who somehow never materialize? Oh, I miss all of it, all right. About as much as I miss winter, and root canal work, and maybe ingrown toenails."

"So, Mr. Hollywood Hotshot, what's your plan for this big-time night in the city of the great, the near-great, and the never-will-be-great?" Ralphie asked.

"I'm torn between the Playboy Mansion, a night out with the Clippers, or maybe hanging with some starlets."

"Betcha that means hiding out in some dump," Plotkin teased, "making the scene with a magazine."

At the sound of some shots fired in the alley behind his motel room, which promptly set off an array of other noises – people screaming, dogs barking, then approaching police sirens – Calvin couldn't help but gaze at his grim and depressing environment.

"I really appreciate your call, guys."

"Any time, homes," Ralphie replied.

"Yeah, any time," Plotkin added. "And please don't forget to give our love to all the women out there – if, that is, you ever manage to meet any."

With the two other Jerseyites laughing, Calvin hung up.

A long way from the Playboy Mansion, or any other sensuous or serious scene, a singularly lonely guy who feared the expense he would likely incur amidst the irresistible used vinyl and CDs at Amoeba Records drove his clunker instead into the Los Feliz area. Then, after a couple of unsuccessful rounds of the heavily trafficked area, Calvin almost miraculously managed to score a parking space.

Into one of the last remaining independent bookstores he stepped, hoping that an hour or so spent browsing would assuage some of his loneliness. But to his dismay, everyone in sight seemed to have some sort of companionship, whether in the form of a significant other or at least a friend or two.

Feeling even more geeky than before, Calvin wandered here and there through the store, occasionally glancing at a novel, a travel book, or a memoir.

But as he approached a section marked *Recent Releases*, he saw a well-dressed guy nearing thirty, and sporting a fashionable stubble, forcefully take a book from the hands of a woman whose back was toward Calvin.

"What gives you the right to tell me what's good and what's not?" Calvin heard the guy ask far too aggressively.

"You're just jealous," was the woman's retort.

"Of what?"

"That one of us can read without her lips moving – and knows that Thomas Pynchon is a novelist, not a pimp or a coke dealer."

His attention having been firmly secured, Calvin listened even more intently as the intensity increased.

"Which one of us has directed films that have grossed over $500 million?" screamed the overly aggressive guy who clearly thought of himself as a hotshot.

"Well, go direct another, because I'm out of here."

The woman made an attempt to leave, but was grabbed around the wrist by the director.

"Says who?" he demanded.

"Says me," answered the woman.

"And me," added Calvin, stepping forward chivalrously.

Seeing red, the hotshot turned on Calvin.

"And who the fuck are you?" he bellowed.

"Just somebody telling you to cool it."

Unaware that taking boxing lessons had become quite the hip thing to do among movie biz up-and-comers, Calvin was unprepared when a roundhouse right, tutored by a trainer at Freddie Roach's Wild Card Gym, nailed him on the chin.

As Calvin started to go down, the hotshot pulled a couple of hundred dollar bills out of his wallet, then tossed them at him.

"Fuck you!" he hollered.

Taking a quick moment to cherish the sight of his KO, the director then stormed off, while the woman bent down to help her fallen would-be rescuer.

"You okay?" she asked

Only at that moment did Calvin realize that instead of some random female, it was a very recognizable woman to whose rescue he had tried to come.

"Either you're J-Jasmine S-Simms," Calvin muttered as he stared at someone whom he had ogled in far too many teen movies while growing up. "Or he hit me harder than I thought."

"And you just did something very silly but brave," Jasmine replied as she helped him to his feet. "Let's go get you some ice."

Still having trouble believing his eyes, Calvin found himself even more dazed when Jasmine gave him an appreciative hug plus a kiss on his cheek – a moment that was captured thanks to several bookstore patrons who had pulled out their iPhones and Androids. Then she led him past a magazine rack where several publications featured cover photos of her.

With an aching jaw compounding all his other problems, another bout of sleeplessness was far from shocking for Calvin, who tossed and turned for a while. Then, after thinking about Jasmine's acting career, he began to compile yet another mental list.

Rather than ruminating about the teen pics that brought Jasmine fame, it was his top ten favorite films that Calvin tried to choose, all the while fully aware that his potential selections separated him even farther from almost all of his contemporaries.

There was not a single chapter of "Star Wars" that was a contender for his personal pantheon. Nor would there be any evidence of Spielberg, including "E.T." Or of John Hughes, whose antiquated (and exclusively white) depictions of teens were as close to Calvin's experiences as life on Pluto or Mars.

He also had reservations about films considered by many critics as pieties: "Lawrence Of Arabia," "The Searchers," Hitchcock's body of work other than "Psycho," and far too much of Chaplin.

To Calvin, American classics were films like Howard Hawks' "His Girl Friday," Billy Wilder's "The Apartment," Robert Rossen's "The Hustler," and Preston Sturges' "The Lady Eve." Plus, of course, "Casablanca" and almost everything ever made by Buster Keaton.

Then there were possibilities that would give some the ammunition to dismiss him as either a culture-vulture or an elitist: "Children Of Paradise," Godard's "Pierrot Le Fou," Resnais' "La Guerre Est Finie," and his favorite 21st century project, the Italian miniseries called "The Best Of Youth." But there was also a taste for what others would consider ridiculously lowbrow: young John Cusack in "Better Off Dead," Joseph Gordon-Levitt in "The Lookout," and an unsung period piece called "Heaven Help Us" set in a Catholic boys high school in Brooklyn.

Even as he finally grew sleepy, Calvin wrestled with other choices as well. Claude Sautet's "Mado" was special to him, and so was Louis Malle's "The Fire Within." Then there were Kurosawa's samurai films, plus Sergio Leone's stupendous "Once Upon A Time In America."

It was while thinking that only Leone could make scenery-chewers like James Woods, Elizabeth McGovern, Burt Young, Treat Williams, and a sometimes somnambulist like Robert DeNiro look like the greatest actors on earth that Calvin finally managed to make the transition into dreamland.

But with his jaw hurting, Sunday was far from a stellar day, with only another trip to the Ethiopian buffet providing any respite from the sense of being alone.

Nor did the night prove to be the slightest bit better as Calvin found himself considering that being ousted from the internship program would probably leave him with the choice of returning with his tail between his legs to his Jersey stomping ground, or alternatively joining the French Foreign Legion, if such a thing still existed.

With little on his *curriculum vitae*, and precious few marketable skills, Calvin could envision little but a life sentence at some dead end job – if, that is, he could even manage to find one.

No surprise then that much of the night was spent in a cold sweat.

Week Two

HARDLY THE BEST-RESTED soul on the planet, Calvin made what had become his customary early morning semi-legal U-turn on Olympic Boulevard. Then his rickety VW followed Jonathan Olson's shiny red Corvette into the Gadzooks parking structure.

Minutes later, feeling even more self-conscious than usual because of the serious bruise he was sporting on his chin, Calvin stepped out of the elevator into the eighth-floor lobby, where Amy Kawasaki and Robert Williams nonetheless ignored him.

Though sorely tempted to say something just to irritate them, Calvin chose instead to play it cool.

Time in the Mail Room that morning seemed to move at a snail's pace, each minute dragging like an hour, each hour feeling almost like a day.

Ready to explode, Calvin burst out from there exactly at noon, then headed straight for I.T., where he barged in like a man gasping for air.

"Tell me we're headed to the park —" Calvin was in the process of blurting when he suddenly realized that instead of being alone, Alonzo was with a very pretty light-skinned woman.

"D-didn't realize you were busy," Calvin mumbled apologetically.

"This is the tofu-toting paleface," Alonzo said to his companion. "Calvin Sands — say hello to the pride of Jamaica, Joy Stewart."

To Calvin's surprise, Joy handed him a brown bag.

"Hope you like rice, beans, and plantains," she said with a smile and a lilting Caribbean accent.

"You didn't have to."

"Trust me," Alonzo stated. "Joy never does anything

because she *has to*."

"Gonna join us?" Calvin asked Joy.

"Wish I could, but duty calls."

"Best music teacher in LA," Alonzo explained.

"Only LA?" Joy joked before turning toward Calvin. "Thanks for feeding my man here the other day."

Calvin watched as Joy kissed Alonzo goodbye, then swung around to face him.

"Hope I see you again," Joy said.

"I hope so, too."

Ten minutes later, gabbing all the way with lunch bags in hand, out from the Gadzooks building came Calvin with Alonzo, who immediately started dribbling his basketball.

"So with that look to your left, look to your right stuff," Calvin said, "do I have any chance in hell of making it?"

"Based on pure percentages?" Alonzo replied. "Nope."

"So why in the world did they bring me in from 3,000 miles away?"

"Truth?"

"Please."

"As filler."

"What's that mean?"

"To put the fear of God into the privileged ones who eventually will make it," Alonzo explained. "Instead of just anointing people, which would give the new hires a sense of what in that world is called *noblesse oblige*, they turn the whole thing into a kind of Kabuki theater."

"By?"

"Bringing in extras to serve as tackling dummies, then announcing that there will be cuts. Clever, huh?"

"In a really perverse, unbelievably shitty way. So I stand zero chance whatsoever?" Calvin asked.

"I didn't say that."

"Then what in the world am I supposed to do?"

Alonzo stopped and faced Calvin.

"What I'm hearing you say is that your Daddy's not a

governor or an ambassador, right?"

"Can't put anything past you."

"Or some ridiculously rich investment banker or oil man."

"Right again."

"And you didn't go to Princeton or Yale."

"Now you've hit the trifecta."

"And, if I'm not incorrect, it just so happens that your family didn't come over on the Mayflower."

"Boy, do you have a keen eye for detail."

"But you tell me, does that stop you from being smarter than the others? Or slicker? Or shrewder?"

Calvin shook his head.

"Then goddamit," insisted Alonzo, raising his voice. "Be smarter! And slicker! And shrewder!"

Having made his point, Alonzo stopped talking and continued walking.

Entering the park in silence, Calvin and Alonzo strode toward one of the picnic benches and put down their lunches.

Once they were seated, Alonzo wasted no time in starting to eat, whereas Calvin sat immobilized.

"What?" Alonzo said finally.

"How exactly do I suddenly start being smarter, slicker, and shrewder?"

"By making use of information."

"What kind of information?"

"Before we get to that," Alonzo said, "why exactly is this so goddamn important to you?"

"Really?"

"Yes, really."

Calvin let out a sigh, which drew a frown from Alonzo.

"That's not an answer," Alonzo stated.

"I was in Jersey, okay? Trying to teach high school biology in a ritzy private school to a bunch of spoiled kids who couldn't give a shit about the difference between a molecule and a mole."

"Why a ritzy private school?"

"Because of a hiring freeze at the inner city school where I thought I could maybe, if I got lucky, make a difference."

"And?"

"So I'm sharing a shithole apartment above a pool hall, with a toilet that backs up every day. And I'm ducking creditors, and living on a diet of bologna, takeout pizza, rice cakes, and nuts."

"Okay —"

"And one day I crack a tooth while chomping on a goddamn almond. So I'm sitting in the dentist's waiting room when I happen to see an article about the founder of Gadzooks."

"The one and only Wesley Phillips."

Calvin nodded.

"And since I've always had this thing about apps, search engines, even algorithms," he went on, "kind of the way some guys fantasize about being Kevin Durant or LeBron or Mick Jagger —"

"And you start seeing the life that our Supreme Master leads —"

"I said to myself —"

"That's who I want to be."

Again Calvin nodded. "Why not for once in my life do more than fantasize or dream?"

"So this time, instead of just fantasizing or dreaming, you take action —"

"Yup."

"And apply for an internship —"

"Right again."

"And when, miracle of miracles, it comes through, you chuck everything —"

"Yes."

"And boogie your butt out here."

"Crazy, huh?" said Calvin with a shrug.

Alonzo studied Calvin for a moment.

"What if I tell you —" Alonzo then began.

"Tell me what?"

"That our buddy Donnelly wants to take a certain female to a convention in Seattle?"

"What's the problem with that?"

"Well, how about we start with the fact that he's married?"

"And?"

"Just his luck, his lovely wife has this burning desire to fly up there with him and see the world famous Space Needle," Alonzo explained.

At 3:15 that afternoon, two interns who happened to be walking down the hall – Jonathan Olson and Samantha Steinberg – paid zero attention when Calvin approached.

But instead of being bugged by the snub, Calvin was totally oblivious, for the simple reason that he was a man with a mission.

Totally focused, he got closer and closer to his destination, then suddenly came to an abrupt stop.

Girding himself, he took a deep breath, steeled himself as best he could, then opened a door that read: MATT DONNELLY – V.P. SALES.

A cute assistant with a name plate on her desk that read *ARIEL* looked up as Calvin stepped in.

"Can I help you?" Ariel asked.

"I-I'd like to see Mr. Donnelly."

"About?"

"A problem."

"And you are?"

"Calvin Sands.

Ariel eyed Calvin strangely, then typed a message.

A moment later, having received a response, she again faced Calvin.

"He says that doesn't ring a bell."

Instead of panicking or bolting, Calvin took a deep breath. "Then please tell him Conrad."

Even more perplexed, Ariel typed another message, then smiled when she got a second response.

"You can go in," she said.

In a room that seemed like a shrine to everything in music that Calvin loathed – memorabilia including a vintage Grateful Dead poster, a signed Neil Diamond album cover, a photo of Billy Joel, plus a shot of Mr. Spiky together with Kenny G, Matt Donnelly, who was on the phone, glanced at Calvin when he opened the door, then gestured for him to enter.

"Okay, dude," Donnelly said into the phone. "I promise... Oh yeah? Not if I see you first."

With a laugh, spiky-haired Donnelly hung up, then glanced at Calvin.

"So, Conrad," he said. "Tell me about this problem."

"To be honest, it's more like I'm kind of a problem solver."

"Okay, I give up. Exactly what kind of problem are you supposed to be solving?"

"I guess you could say it deals with personnel," Calvin replied.

"Personnel, huh?"

"Or maybe you could say it goes under travel."

"And who, if you don't mind my asking, is having this problem you're referring to?"

"From what I've been hearing, you."

"What the fuck are you talking about?" Donnelly asked.

"Helping you get what you want in Seattle."

Based on the look Donnelly gave him in response, Calvin could not help but feel that his days at Gadzooks had just come to an abrupt and unhappy end.

Then suddenly a gleam appeared in Matt Donnelly's eyes, one that made it clear he somehow had finally begun to grasp what Calvin was suggesting.

"Something tells me, Conrad," Donnelly then announced with what Calvin took to be rather dimwitted, but nonetheless gleeful, anticipation, "that I've been short-changing you."

Feeling significantly better about both the world and his place in it, Calvin was approaching the entrance of Cash &

Carrie a few minutes later when the door swung open and, much to his astonishment, out stepped none other than Wesley Phillips, holding a takeout latte.

"Morning, Mr. Phillips," Calvin said tentatively, causing Phillips to stop in his tracks and eye him.

"You part of our team?"

"I'm a new intern."

"Then call me Wes."

Not knowing how to respond, Calvin watched in respectful and somewhat awed silence as the legendary founder of the internet giant patted him on the shoulder, then headed off.

With significantly more confidence than usual, plus a decided spring in his step, Calvin entered the little restaurant and smiled at May, then sauntered up to the counter, where Carrie was at her usual post.

"You know that was the head of Gadzooks who just left?" he said.

"Maybe I should put up a plaque," Carrie replied. "Or even better, seal the area and call a press conference."

"I didn't mean –"

"I know. It's just that if it were Marcel Duchamp. Or the Buddha. Or maybe Ray Charles."

"They're all dead."

"Just my luck. So what can I do you for?"

"Well –"

"Is that *well* as in I'd like a donut?" Carrie asked. "Or *well* as in how about a hot fudge sundae?"

"Actually, it was *well* as in something good just happened. So I was hoping I could celebrate by maybe taking you to a ball game. Or if you'd rather, buying you dinner."

"And then top off the good news by trying to win that pool?"

"N-not what I was thinking," said Calvin, who was suddenly unsettled.

"Listen, umm –"

"Calvin."

"I appreciate the offer. But I've got this thing about guys I meet through work."

Carrie was suddenly distracted when May stepped toward her and asked a question in Mandarin, which Carrie answered in the same language. Then, with a shrug, Calvin spoke up.

"It doesn't really have to be a date-date."

"Tell you what," said Carrie gently. "How about a piece of apple pie a la mode? And because you're sweet, it's on me."

Though still far from joyful, Calvin's afternoon, thanks to the hope instilled during his meeting with Donnelly, proved to be dramatically less painful than the day before.

But due to his failure with Carrie, the evening found him all alone, unhappily ensconced in Motel Hell, where he was killing time on his iPad when the cell phone rang.

"Aren't I a lucky guy?" he said, having once again recognized the Caller ID.

"Dog!" Plotkin, at the wheel of his Volvo, bellowed through the wonders of Bluetooth. "I owe you an apology."

"For what?" Calvin asked.

"For what?! Here we were thinking you were at home every night beating your meat —"

"Spanking your monkey —" Ralphie chimed in.

"Making the scene with a magazine —"

"And instead," added Ralphie, "you were getting there!"

"Doin' it!"

"Jammin'!"

"What in hell are you fools talking about?" Calvin asked.

"Our dream girl!" Ralphie yelled.

"From *The World's Hippest High School*."

"And *Mimi Goes To College*!"

"And *Everybody Loves Lucy Quinn*!"

"Please give me this in English," Calvin pleaded.

"You and Jasmine!" Plotkin explained.

"Jasmine Simms, my dream girl since that scene in her underwear when we were back in middle school!" Ralphie added.

"How do you know about that?" Calvin asked.

"You kidding?" replied Plotkin. "All of North Jersey knows!"

"But how?"

"You two are in the paper!" Ralphie shouted.

And even though Calvin could not possibly see over the phone, Ralphie tried to prove his point by holding up a copy of the Newark Star Ledger, which featured a photo of Calvin and Jasmine Simms on the front page, accompanied by a headline that read: *Local Boy Scores In Hollywood!*

"Check it out yourself on the internet," Plotkin said.

"And even better, ask her if she's got friends," Ralphie interjected.

"What for?"

"Because one of these days," Plotkin promised, "your homies are coming out that way for a visit."

All Calvin could do was groan.

At 4:20 the next afternoon, with the suspense mounting as to when the first "execution" of an intern would take place, the Mail Room was divided into its usual configuration, Rolando Dango and Samantha Steinberg sorting a pile of correspondence together, while Robert Williams sat off to one side, and Calvin worked alone on the other.

Then in stepped Amy Kawasaki, who moseyed her way arrogantly toward Calvin.

"Guess who Mr. Spiky wants to see," she said patronizingly.

The others watched Calvin leave the room, then turned to Amy.

"This mean what I think it means?" asked Robert.

Before Amy could answer, Samantha, who was already gloating, patted Rolando on the back.

"Something tells me you and I have just won the pool," she announced.

Too intrigued to sit patiently and wait, the interns

collectively departed from the Mail Room so as to get the truth as soon as possible.

Though seemingly engrossed in work on his laptop, Matt Donnelly looked up with a smile when the door was opened by Calvin.

"There's my man!" Donnelly exclaimed.

After getting up and greeting Calvin with a warm handshake, Donnelly closed the door, then led him in.

"So we're fine as wine? Good as wood?" Donnelly asked.

"Nice as –" Calvin thought for a moment, "– ice."

"And this, of course, stays one hundred percent between us?"

"I'm just trying to do my best to help."

"And, as I hope you realized, scoring big, big points."

"I'm a team player, Mr. Donnelly."

"Matt," Donnelly insisted, drawing an okay in the form of a nod from Calvin.

"The way things work," Donnelly then went on, "is that while the people attending the conference are meeting, there are all sorts of programs – to use today's parlance – for the spouses and significant others: tennis, spa treatment, speakers, and that kind of shit. Which means that by day, my wife will happily be very, very busy."

"And so will you."

Donnelly beamed. "Thanks, that is, to a certain resourceful intern. So your job is to take notes at the different meetings –"

"And babysit at night?"

"My man is getting it!" exclaimed Donnelly.

But Donnelly's jubilation came to an abrupt halt when his intercom suddenly buzzed.

Quickly, he grabbed his desk phone. "What?" he asked, his smile turning immediately turning to a frown. "Okay..."

Hanging up, Donnelly, his mood having significantly darkened, gathered himself, then turned once more to Calvin.

"Time to be cool, okay?"

Without waiting for a response, Donnelly marched toward his office door and opened it as a woman who could easily pass as the national leader in chipperness entered.

"Goosie!" the ebullient woman with short auburn hair and bright red nail polish chirped.

"Cupcake!" Donnelly responded.

The two of them hugged, then the woman glanced at Calvin.

"I'm the other half of the team known as Matt and Katt," she merrily announced.

"This is Conrad," Donnelly said by way of introduction. "He's the guy who'll be coming to Seattle with a lady friend."

Katt wasted no time in going into a well-rehearsed pitch.

"Does she know about NewSkin?" she inquired merrily.

"Newskin?" asked Calvin.

Katt instantly pulled some fliers out from her purse.

"Best product in the whole wide world for facial care," she gushed as she handed the paperwork to Calvin. "Always remember, when a woman feels good about her face, you can bet she's ready to face the world!"

Feeling uncomfortable, Donnelly tapped Calvin on the shoulder.

"Don't you have a staff meeting?" he asked.

"A w-what?" Calvin muttered. "Oh, right."

Calvin smiled at Katt, then started for the door, not realizing that Mrs. Donnelly was still in selling mode.

"Maybe the four of us can have dinner in Seattle," Katt said.

"I... uhh... have a feeling I'll be pretty darn busy," Calvin mumbled.

In the hallway outside Donnelly's office, the interns from the Mail Room — Samantha, Robert, Rolando, and Amy — having been joined by fellow vulture Jonathan Olson, AKA Mr. Oil Spill, hovered while waiting for fresh prey.

Convinced that carrion would soon be theirs, they nearly pounced when the door opened and Calvin emerged.

"So?" asked Samantha impatiently.

"Did they can your ass?" Jonathan demanded.

"What's the bottom line?" Robert blurted.

Savoring the situation, Calvin took a moment to eye each and every one of them individually, then shrugged.

"Well, in some ways it's an imposition."

"What kind of imposition?" Samantha asked.

"Well –" Calvin said, milking the moment.

"C'mon, man! What do you have to do?" pushed Jonathan.

"Yeah!" added Robert.

"Take a business trip," Calvin said with a smile.

Giving no further explanation, Calvin sauntered merrily away, leaving the others in a state of total confusion and – if the truth be known – disappointment.

At 12:30 the next day, up to the park that served as their midday sanctuary came Alonzo and Calvin, armed with lunches and their basketball.

"But even so, you're worried?" Alonzo asked, continuing a conversation that was already in progress.

"Worried?" Calvin muttered. "I'm way beyond just worried. What I'm doing – what I'm about to do – hell, I don't even have a clue what to call it."

"How about chaperoning? Or helping out? Or maybe just moving up the corporate ladder?"

"Those are just euphemisms."

"That's a pretty big word from an intern who not all that long ago was convinced he'd be getting axed."

The two of them reached their usual picnic table, where Alonzo put down his basketball and took a seat.

"Then what exactly am I?" Calvin asked.

"You want the appropriate term?"

"Yes, please."

"Ready?"

"Ready."

"Sure?"

"Yes, I'm sure!"

"Calvin my man, you're –"

"Yeah?"

"The Beard."

Calvin allowed himself a moment or two to ponder Alonzo's words, then nodded without an abundance of mirth.

Alonzo, however, was not quite finished.

"But that's not enough," he said. "What you're doing – or are about to do?"

"Okay –"

"It can't be just to help a doofus like Donnelly. You dig? You gotta –"

When Alonzo failed to finish his sentence, Calvin nearly burst.

"Gotta what?" he demanded.

"Find some ways to score points for the home team."

"What in hell does that mean?"

"While you're there," Alonzo said firmly, "you've also gotta do everything imaginable – every goddamn thing possible – to help the home team, which means you."

With the other interns still trying desperately to figure out what in the world could have possibly transpired in Matt Donnelly's office, the rest of the afternoon was strangely amusing for Calvin. Instead of being ignored, he found himself the recipient of overtures the likes of which he had never before experienced or expected. Amy Kawasaki, for one, made a point of gracing him a smile when they passed in the hall. Imran Habib, who until then had been nothing but distant, surprised him in the men's room with a surprisingly collegial, "Guess we're still here." And Harley Brooks, who had never been the least bit unpleasant, made a point of approaching him near the coffee machine to say, "I love seeing you make the shitheads sweat."

Feeling considerably better about himself, his situation, and above all his newly improved chances, Calvin not surprisingly found his post-work commute far less painful than it had been before. And the dinnertime tacos more tasty than usual. And the cacophony outside Motel Hell significantly less disturbing.

Sleep, however, came no more easily than in previous nights. The difference was that instead of all purpose woes – *Who am I? What will become of me? Was my trip west for naught?* – it was something far more specific that gnawed at Calvin: *What have I gotten myself into?* Then there was another key question. Once the weekend gets under way, he wondered while contemplating Alonzo's advice, *How do I find a way to do everything possible – or even anything at all – to help myself?*

He thought of making yet another list, but had trouble deciding on a topic until he found himself thinking of all the Otis Redding song titles he could name. Starting with "Dock Of The Bay" and "Try A Little Tenderness," he went through "I've Been Loving You Too Long," "Respect," and "These Arms Of Mine," then finally conked out after "Pain In My Heart."

Early Friday afternoon, down a San Fernando Valley street lined with nondescript apartment buildings, many with *For Rent* and *Vacancy* signs, came a Lincoln Town Car, which swung into a space marked *Passenger Loading*. Then out from the back seat stepped a guy who was clearly ill at ease.

Wondering what he had gotten himself into, Calvin thought for a moment about joining the circus, enlisting in the Marines, or fleeing to Mexico, then girded himself and approached the four-story building ahead of him.

Moments later, an elevator door opened on the third floor, then out stepped Calvin. Straightening his clothes, he trudged down the hall in search of the appropriate apartment, then wiped his sweaty brow and took a deep breath in the hope of calming his nerves. Recognizing it was do or die, he finally rang the doorbell.

A moment passed, then another, before the door was opened by a young blonde who looked like she would have no clue whatsoever as to the meaning of the word *cynicism*, let alone how to spell it, even if her life depended on it.

Wholesomeness, for Calvin, had always seemed like little more than an abstraction, or maybe a quality from some mythic past. Yet the glorious creature greeting him with a smile seemed to be the very personification of wholesome.

"You must be Conrad!" she gushed.

"Calvin."

"And I'm Daisy. This is so nice of you."

"Happy to help."

"Let me just grab my suitcase."

"Allow me."

"Aren't you the gentleman?" Daisy chirped.

Emerging from the apartment building together with Calvin, Daisy responded with a sense of wonder when she spotted the Lincoln Town Car, whose driver, sporting a name tag that said *Jose*, was standing beside the open trunk.

"Ooh golly," Daisy exclaimed. "You must be important."

"Not really."

"C'mon, with a car like that?"

Jose the chauffeur opened the trunk, then surreptitiously eyeballed Daisy while taking the suitcase from Calvin.

Assuming her to be Calvin's date, Jose gave him a stealthy wink of approval, then scurried to open the back doors.

Side by side in the spacious back seat, Daisy and Calvin watched Jose climb behind the wheel. As the Lincoln began its journey toward the airport, Daisy turned to her seatmate with a sweet smile.

"So we're weekend roomies, huh?"

"Guess you could say that."

"And I bet you've flown before."

Calvin nodded. "And you?"

"I'm a virgin," Daisy said sheepishly, immediately starting to blush. "Well," she then added, "not entirely."

Instead of responding, Calvin made believe he didn't hear the comment.

A couple of minutes of silence ensued. But as the Town Car turned onto the 405 Freeway, Daisy again faced Calvin.

"So you and Matt are work buddies?" she asked.

"I guess you could more or less kind of say that. So tell me, how did the two of you meet?"

"It's a little embarrassing."

"How so?"

"It was because of a flat tire."

"Did he change it for you?"

"Not exactly," Daisy said.

"Which means?"

"He was waiting for the Auto Club on Ventura Boulevard on Saturday afternoon, looking all forlorn and stuff."

"And?"

"So I kinda rolled up my sleeves – even though I was actually wearing a tank top – and changed it for him."

"You changed his tire?"

"And I can change spark plugs, tune an engine, fix a crankcase –"

"For real?"

"When your daddy is a long-distance trucker," Daisy said after smiling proudly, "there's all kinds of neat and useful stuff you learn."

Kicking himself for having jumped prematurely to a conclusion about Daisy, Calvin began to see his new companion in an entirely different light.

The flight, which Calvin had feared would be an exasperating exercise in babysitting, proved to be anything but. Thanks to Daisy's ebullience, plus her strange blend of innocence in certain realms, but expertise in others, Calvin found himself strangely charmed.

Though blissfully unaware of the kinds of films, books, and records that Calvin revered, and willfully oblivious to all forms of politics, she was both knowledgeable and passionate about farm animals, incredibly interested in ecology and environmental issues, and surprisingly articulate about the trials and tribulations of the working poor.

Beyond charmed, Calvin found himself embarrassed because of his initial judgment of her as a yokel or a ditz. And on top of everything, he loved the fact that she originally hailed from a town whose name he at first assumed to be a joke: Toad Suck Ferry, Arkansas.

Calvin's reassessment of Daisy soon led to another, more troubling, form of distress. Despite his awareness that she was a grown-up, and a willing and eager participant in the weekend plans, he nonetheless found himself feeling both guilty and ill-at-ease about his involvement.

Had Daisy been only a bimbo, simply a bimbo, nothing more than a bimbo, everything would have been far, far simpler. But in truth, she was adorable, sweet, and wonderful. Which meant that nothing in Calvin's life was either as straightforward or as easy as he hoped it would be.

At the airport in Seattle, another Lincoln Town Car awaited, with a chauffeur who took their luggage, then drove them to the Grand Hyatt.

There the two of them were greeted with effusiveness at the check-in desk, then led by a bellhop to a room with a spectacular view of the Space Needle, plus a king size bed.

Acting as though all this was commonplace for him, Calvin tipped the bellhop, who promptly left, closing the door behind him. Then came a shrug as he faced Daisy.

"I don't know why they gave us only one bed," Calvin said somewhat apologetically.

"Because, silly, they think we're a couple."

"Hungry?" Calvin asked, trying to change the subject.

"You know, you don't really have to babysit."

"What if I'd like some company?"

Daisy gave him a smile he wished he could package and save.

"Mind if I shower first?" she then asked. "After a morning of toting eggs and bacon, then a lunch serving burgers, milkshakes, and fries –"

Calvin nodded, so Daisy walked into the bathroom and turned on the shower, then started to disrobe without closing the door, affording Calvin what he found to be a rather staggering view.

"Okay, if I close the door?" he mumbled with no small amount of embarrassment.

"But it'll get so steamy."

"Daisy, you're killing me."

"C'mon, you never went skinny-dipping?"

Calvin made a serious attempt to be calm, but that was a state of being that he was in no way able to reach.

"I think I'm gonna go run ten miles or so," he muttered in defeat.

"You run that much?"

"Almost never."

Calvin's run through an unfamiliar city was less an opportunity to see sights than an attempt to diminish the desire that was coursing through his body, while simultaneously silencing the thoughts running through his mind.

Neither goal, however, was accomplished. Even as he grew more and more weary, the memory of Daisy's nubile body proved sufficient to sustain his libido. His mind, meanwhile, kept fixating on one theme: *What in hell have I gotten myself into?*

The answer, Calvin tried repeatedly to convince himself, was not to ponder the morality of what he was doing, nor to reflect on what it said about him. The goal, instead, was to figure out how he could at least get something out of the bizarre pickle into which he had somehow gotten himself.

Matt and Katt Donnelly were stepping out of the Grand Hyatt when Calvin, sweaty and winded from his run, came lumbering up.

"There's my man!" bellowed Donnelly. "Everything good?"

"Peachy," Calvin replied, though such was hardly the case.

"Cool," said Donnelly, shooting Calvin a conspiratorial wink.

Unlocking the door to his hotel room minutes later, Calvin was surprised to find a barbequed chicken pizza sitting in front of Daisy who, looking almost edible in a skin-tight Willie Nelson T-shirt, was busily studying a map of Seattle.

"Hope you don't mind," she said, "but I took it upon myself to set up an itinerary. Can I tell you?"

"Sure."

"This is our snack for now. Then we'll take the walking tour I scoped out, stop at a place that sounds great for a pre-dinner drink, and finally feed our faces at a little French bistro that sounds cute and funky. That okay?"

"Sounds perfect."

"Except?" Daisy asked.

"What do you mean, except?"

"I feel like there's something you're holding back."

"Well —"

"Well, what?"

"You don't by any chance —"

"What?"

"Have a twin sister?" Calvin said.

"You're sweet," Daisy said as she hoisted a slice of pizza.

Both on their stroll and then over dinner, Calvin was vividly aware of what seemed like the countless glances, looks, and stares that came his way. From men, the dominant emotion was envy, based on the presumption that he was more than a simply a chaste companion for Daisy. From women came something new and far more profound: the kind of luster that derived from the assumption that he must be someone particularly special to be involved with such an absolute knockout.

The result was that at dinner, he found himself becoming strangely peevish. When the waitress mispronounced a wine that Calvin remembered discussing in a college French class, he went overboard by first correcting her, then making her repeat his pronunciation. Then, despite Daisy's queasiness, he ordered escargots for an appetizer. And finally, when she asked for a translation of a dish called *Chevreuil a la Sauce Poivrade*, he gave her a one-word answer: "Bambi."

But instead of making him feel better, his behavior instead made him embarrassed. Daisy, he knew full well, deserved better than the ridiculous petulance he was stupidly manifesting.

It was nearing 11 PM when back to the Grand Hyatt, with no afterglow whatsoever, came Calvin and Daisy. Despite the looks that came their way, it was with zero glee that they hoofed across the lobby, then climbed into an elevator.

Once in the room, modesty prevailed as the two of them took turns getting ready for bed. Then, awkwardly, they climbed under the covers and turned off the lights.

A moment passed, then another, before Daisy leaned toward Calvin.

"You awake?" she whispered.

"Yup."

"You know that salad you ate?"

"Yeah?"

"Were they really the hearts of small rodents?"

"I was just teasing."

"Honest?"

"Artichokes are a vegetable."

"Really?"

"Really," Calvin said. "And you know what? I apologize."

"Hey, an artichoke is no big thing."

"But my behavior is. I don't know what I was doing."

"Being a guy," Daisy stated.

"I guess you're right."

"Well, apology accepted."

"Thanks."

Relieved, Daisy reached over and kissed Calvin on the cheek.

"I can sleep now," she said with a sigh. "You, too?"

"I'll try."

"C'mon –"

"C'mon, what?"

"A guy as successful as you must have girls beating down your door."

Instead of responding, Calvin tried to will himself into dreamland. But as Daisy began to snore ever so sweetly, Calvin recognized that sleep, for him, was hardly in the cards.

He tossed and turned in a futile attempt to find a comfortable place for himself, all the while far too vividly aware of Daisy's warm and inviting body beside him.

Inevitably, Calvin decided to resort to his usual list-making, with his first impulse being an urge to think of the women – past and present – with whom he would most like to have sex. But thoughts about Bridget Bardot, Marilyn Monroe, a young Debbie Harry, Beyonce, and Anna Karina, instead of inducing sleep, instead made him even more hot and bothered.

Abruptly he changed direction and began coming up with places he'd day love to visit some day, starting with Paris, Havana, Bangkok, and the country of Nepal.

But when that attempt, too, brought him no closer to sleep, Calvin tried to fight what had become a nearly overwhelming sense of desire by making believe he was first LeBron James, then Russell Westbrook, then bearded James Hardin, dominating opponents in NBA playoff games.

That, however, also proved to be monumentally ineffective.

Troubled by his inability to sleep, plus what had become an impossible to ignore horniness, Calvin got up and tiptoed into the bathroom, where just his luck he found Daisy's bra and panties hanging up to dry.

To keep from being overwhelmed, he grabbed his running shoes again as he prepared to jog another three or four miles.

Early the next morning, with Daisy still fast asleep, Calvin got up and took another shower, then dressed quietly and slipped out of the room.

Stricken with a case of performance anxiety, he went downstairs to the coffee shop and did his best to calm his nerves first with orange juice, eggs, and toast, then with a Red Bull, before heading toward the hotel's Pavilion Room, where a banner heralded *THE FUTURE OF TELECOMMUNICATIONS.*

Taking a moment to get his bearings, Calvin diffidently approached the Sign-In desk, where several eager beavers were handling registrations. After a deep breath, he walked up to a redhead with a name tag that said *Joni.*

"I-I'm from Gadzooks," Calvin mumbled despite his eagerness to sound confident.

"Mr. Donnelly?" Joni asked.

"Sands," Calvin corrected.

Overhearing, a patrician-looking Brit with a Saville Row suit leaned toward Calvin.

"A changing of the guard?" he asked.

"After a fashion."

Instantly, the Englishman extended a hand. "Nigel Caton-Pratt, Auracall U.K."

"Calvin Sands."

Both men took a moment to get their ID's, which were attached to cords that they put around their necks, then together they started toward where the activities were about to get under way.

"So tell me about the Dating App," Caton-Pratt said hopefully.

Instead of admitting his own ignorance, Calvin made a split-second decision to play it cool – or as cool as someone who felt he was in over his head could manage to make it seem.

"W-what's there to say?" Calvin offered.

"Coy, huh?" replied the Brit, misconstruing Calvin's stutter.

"Not really."

"Come now –"

"What if I tell you I have absolutely no idea?"

Caton-Pratt chuckled.

"I'm beginning to see why they sent you instead of that foolish blabbermouth Donnelly," he responded. "Let's cut right to the chase, shall we? Are you willing to grant an exclusive?"

"Really, I'm not at liberty –"

"So we're playing hard to get, are we? May I have your card?"

"D-didn't bring one."

Caton-Pratt eyed Calvin for a moment, then chortled.

"Smashing, dear boy!" he exclaimed. "I think you're about to see that I can be persistence personified."

Both of them took seats just in time to hear the first speaker.

Moments later, sleep-deprived Calvin found himself fighting to stay awake.

At the mid-morning break, a still drowsy Calvin grabbed a cup of coffee. In the hope of getting some air, he stepped outside the Grand Hyatt just in time to catch sight of two familiar figures – Matt Donnelly and Daisy – climbing into a cab.

Grimacing, Calvin pulled out his iPhone, then heard a recognizable British voice approaching.

"There you are!" said Nigel Caton-Pratt, shuffling swiftly toward him. "Whether or not a worldwide exclusive is a possibility, whatever you're expecting for Ireland, Scotland, and even Jamaica, plus of course jolly old England – we're prepared to better it."

"Mr. Caton-Pratt –"

"Please, dear boy, Nigel. And no evasiveness, shall we? The improved Date-Dialing must – and shall indeed – be ours. Straight, Gay, Bi-, Transgender, the whole – how do you say? – empanada."

"Enchilada," Calvin corrected, aware that whether through luck, fate, or fluke, he may have stumbled upon a way to make Alonzo's advice a reality.

With no great interest in the rest of the speakers, Calvin decided to quit while he was ahead, rather than risk further hounding by Nigel. So, without a word to anyone, he grabbed a map from the hotel's concierge, then embarked on a walking tour of Seattle.

The Space Needle was his first destination, followed by Pike Place Market, then a visit to a chocolate factory – each excursion punctuated by a stop, over several hours, at three different coffee houses.

All the while, Calvin did his best to avoid any thought of what Daisy and Donnelly might be up to.

As evening neared, Calvin flirted with the notion of forgoing his babysitting duty by hiding out in a dive bar, only to realize that shirking responsibility or ducking would not merely be cowardly, but also ineffective. No amount of gin, tequila, or even boilermakers, he knew too well, would be sufficient to silence the thoughts that were running this way and that through his mind.

The dinner with Daisy, which took place at a funky but congenial Thai restaurant, proved to be awkward, strained, and filled with extended gaps in which neither person seemed able to find the right words to express all that went unsaid.

Uncomfortably, the two of them ultimately made their way back to the Grand Hyatt. There, somewhat together in body, but certainly not in spirit, they made it through the rest of the evening by watching "Double Indemnity" on a local station, then washed up and climbed tentatively into bed.

Separated by inches physically, but by miles in every other way, they turned off the lights in the hope that sleep would bring some semblance of respite or solace. But such was not to be the case.

Side by side, each of them stared at the ceiling as time seemed to stop. Then finally Daisy spoke.

"You might as well ask," she said.

"Ask what?"

"What's been on your mind since the moment we met.'"

"Namely?"

"Why?"

"I don't follow," Calvin mumbled.

"Like hell, you don't. You're either too shy, or well-mannered, or maybe just plain nice to ask why in the world I said yes to Matt."

"It's really none of my business."

"As sweet as you've been with me? Think it's easy to be away from family and friends, worrying about the rent, gas, and all the other expenses every single month? And having nine million guys – and sometimes not just guys – trying to get a piece of you? It's not like Matt's some kind of Prince Charming or anything. But at least he's never hustled me, or fed me any corny promises or lines. This was a chance to get away, see something new, and most of all to make believe, if only for a couple of days, that I was part of a world that didn't feel like the last stop on a train to Nowhereville. If that makes me a terrible person, then you know what? I can live with it."

"C'mon," Calvin said. "If there's a terrible person in this room, it's me."

"For trying to get somewhere? In a world where people lie, cheat, and steal? Then I've got news for you. As a bad person, sorry – you don't begin to qualify. And please don't try to contradict me. Know why?"

"I give up?"

"Because," Daisy said, "not only does yours truly know how to work on cars, but I also studied karate. So if you ever get in a pinch and need a bodyguard –"

After a laugh, the two of them, relaxed at last, soon fell asleep.

The flight to Los Angeles the next day at noon, though by no means a gab fest, was curiously comfortable, with Daisy and Calvin both experiencing the warmth that comes from having survived a shared crucible. And when Daisy leaned over and fell asleep on his shoulder, Calvin felt both happy and proud.

Met at the airport by Jose and the Lincoln, they immediately headed off toward Daisy's neighborhood.

Once they reached her building, Calvin got out of the car to give her a hug, then vows were made to stay in touch, even though both of them knew how unlikely that was.

Alone in the back seat as the Town Car headed toward his motel, Calvin suddenly found himself feeling strangely, profoundly, alarmingly alone.

His life, as he thought about it, seemed remarkably, distressingly, bizarrely free of what he termed cause-and-effect. No experience, whether good, bad, or indifferent, led directly or even indirectly to any lasting change, whether quantitative or qualitative. No matter what he did, or what he tried, he always seemed to wind up in a situation that required starting over.

Alone again at Motel Hell, Calvin found himself pondering what he'd been through not just in Seattle, but also across the span of what he considered to be his life.

As the evening went on, however, those concerns segued into speculation about what might lie ahead.

But after a while, what exactly his future might hold began to seem less of an issue than whether, in any real of meaningful sense, he even had a future.

Once more sleep did not come easily to Calvin.

Week Three

BRIGHT AND EARLY Monday morning, Calvin stepped out of the Gadzooks parking lot and headed toward the entrance to Cash & Carrie for a dose of badly needed caffeine, only to find a smiling Matt Donnelly standing there.

"Thought I might find you here," Donnelly said, extending a hand. "I owe you, buddy-boy."

"Hey –"

"Hey, my ass! You came through for me, and don't you dare think I'll forget it. But one thing –"

"Yeah?"

"That deal with Nigel?"

"Uh-huh?"

"Let's keep it between you and me."

"Whatever you say, Mr. Donnelly."

"Matt," Donnelly insisted.

As Donnelly gave Calvin a hug, out from Cash & Carrie, with a container of take-out coffee in hand, stepped Harlan Brooks III. Harley waited silently until the embrace was over. Then, once Donnelly was headed toward the building's main entrance, he approached Calvin.

"Looks like somebody's gonna make some interns I know even more jealous," Harley said.

"Including you?"

"Shit, man. I got no more feeling for those tools than you do. But don't be surprised if some of 'em are really pissed – and others start suckin' up to you big time."

Patting Calvin on the shoulder, Harley headed off to work.

A few minutes later, Alonzo Stevens emerged from the inner offices into the reception area of the Gadzooks offices. Pad in hand, he was on his way toward the door when in stepped Calvin, with a bran muffin and some coffee.

"One step closer to the goal line?" Alonzo asked.

"Thanks to you," Calvin replied.

"Follow football?"

"More or less."

"Well, there's this funny thing about how things work," Alonzo continued. "Even if a quarterback throws a perfect pass—"

"Yeah?"

"Ain't nothing positive happens unless the receiver catches the ball. Rumor has it you did good. See you at lunch?"

"Wouldn't miss it for the world," Calvin said.

At 10:20 that morning, with rumors flying about imminent firings, which in turn led to higher and higher tension amongst the interns, a none-too-happy Imran Habib plodded his way down the corridor, then opened the door to the Mail Room.

Ignoring the other denizens, he approached Calvin.

"Mr. In-Demand," Imran announced, "it seems your presence is requested in Product Development."

Robert Williams, who took time over the weekend to have his hair bleached blond, was unable to keep his curiosity in check.

"By whom?" he asked.

"Mark Zuckerberg."

"Very funny."

Paying no attention to the back and forth, Calvin sauntered out of the Mail Room, causing Robert to fume.

"Who really?" he demanded.

"George Kim," Imran answered.

"The Number Two man in the fucking department?" Robert wailed before striding toward the wall and banging his fist against it.

"Somebody's jealous," Samantha stated.

"And something tells me I'm far from the only one!" Robert screamed.

Entering the Product Development suite, Calvin approached the receptionist, who had bright red lipstick and multiple piercings.

"I'm —" Calvin started to say, only to be interrupted

immediately.

"The rising young star," the receptionist, who preferred to go by Sunshine rather than her given name of Margaret, replied, beating him to the punch.

Seeing Calvin's surprise, Sunshine swiftly offered an explanation. "Word spreads fast at a place I call Gossip Central. Wander on in. *El Jefe* impatiently awaits your arrival."

An athletic-looking Korean-American in his mid-30's, George Kim looked up with a smile as Calvin opened the door to his office.

"Come on in," said Kim, who rose so as to shake Calvin's hand, then headed over to close the door behind him. "Sit."

Calvin did as requested while George Kim stepped back behind his desk.

"I understand you've got aspirations," Kim stated.

"Doesn't everyone?"

"Aspirations? Yes. A sense of reality? Questionable. And as for resourcefulness, ingenuity, and the good sense to be tight-lipped? Far too rare indeed. So tell me a little about Seattle."

"Damp but nice."

"And the conference?"

"Interesting."

"Interesting, my sweet Asian ass!" Kim bellowed with a laugh. "If that kind of shit's interesting, then I'm LeBron James. So let's talk turkey, huh? Tell me how you closed with Nigel."

"I beg your pardon."

"Am I hearing somebody protecting Donnelly?"

Calvin made no effort to respond.

"Look, I love loyalty," Kim stated, "but in this case there's not a chance in hell it's going to fly. The bottom line about Donnelly? A two-faced toad who has trouble finding his own dick in the dark. Am I right?"

Still, Calvin said nothing.

"So why's he here, you're wondering," Kim went on. "Let's just say that at one point someone in his family did a solid for Wesley Phillips, okay? And Wesley Phillips, so that you know, is not a guy who forgets. We on the same page?"

"I-I guess."

"I don't want Donnelly leaning on you again and again for favors. And furthermore, I'm prepared to make it known that it was you – not that glad-handing moron – who delivered the Aurocall deal. We clear?"

Calvin's only response was a nod.

"Then, since it seems you're the king of discretion," Kim stated, "there's one important question that needs to be asked. Ready?"

"I guess."

"What are you up to this weekend?" George Kim asked.

Seeing another rung on the corporate ladder start to materialize, Calvin smiled.

"You tell me," he said.

A cluster of interns whose emotions ranged the gamut from curiosity to thinly-veiled envy and on to blatant jealousy – Jonathan, Samantha, Robert, Rolando, and Imran – were hovering restlessly in the corridor outside the Product Development suite when out stepped Calvin, who thwarted their quest for answers by sauntering off quickly in the other direction.

While his fellow interns stood frozen, Jonathan Olson wasted not a second before scurrying after Calvin.

"Yo, bro!" he shouted. "Wait up!"

Calvin, however, made zero effort to heed, so Jonathan sped up.

"I was thinking, my man," he continued. "How about lunch today at the Bel Air Bay Club?"

"I'm booked," Calvin replied.

"Then what do you say to something this weekend?"

Calvin stopped on a dime and faced his new-found suitor.

"I'll be on a business trip," he announced proudly.

At lunchtime, again toting a basketball in addition to their lunches, Alonzo and Calvin, having made their daily escape from Gadzooks, strode into their favorite retreat in mid-conversation.

"I don't get it," Alonzo said as they entered the park. "You were worried when nothing was going right, and now you're worried because everything's going right?"

"I also worry because a day is Sunday, or Monday, or Tuesday," Calvin joked. "And whether God exists. And why little kids get cancer, but guys like Dick Cheney go unpunished."

"Somebody's getting philosophical and political."

"Bother you?"

"Hell, no! My take is simple, "Alonzo said. "It's too bad there's disaster on this earth. But since it exists, why can't I be the one to pick who it hits? But instead of all-purpose worries and woes, let's talk about yours."

"This roller coaster ride I'm on –"

"Yeah?"

"Anybody been on it before?"

"Yup."

"Successfully?"

"Well, there was Ruderman."

"And did he score?"

"He was on the heavy-duty fast track when a huge Texas firm swooped in and stole him away."

"No shit?"

"Calvin, it was like the entire world was his."

"Was?"

"Yup."

"And where's he now?" Calvin asked.

"Honestly?"

"Of course."

"Leavenworth," Alonzo replied, drawing a gasp from Calvin.

"L-Leavenworth P-Prison?"

"You got it."

"B-but how?" Calvin asked. "And why?"

"Long version or short?"

"Let's start with short."

"He was Senior VP at Enron."

Though a part of him remained apprehensive – and, he recognized, probably always would – Calvin found that instead of an all-enveloping kind of dread, what he began to feel was a less troubling but far too familiar sense of uncertainty. For as long as he could remember, the flip side of joy was the sense that it was doomed to be finite, which meant that the *down* that would follow would be at least commensurate with, and perhaps worse than, whatever *up* he had just happened to experience. *Good*, therefore, came to be perceived as nothing more than the prelude to *bad*. That could mean, for instance, going from the bliss of his grandmother's house to the incessant grief that emanated from his mother, whose harping and criticizing reached an apotheosis in an angry remark Calvin would never forget: "Don't look at me in that tone of voice!"

Or it could mean having a great game during his time playing high school basketball, yet realizing that at his size he had no foreseeable future in a sport that he loved. Or it could be as simple as trucking into New York to see someone like Bobby "Blue" Bland or Sonny Rollins, then recognizing that despite whatever glow he'd gotten from the performance, he would once again wake up the next morning feeling trapped.

Despite the misgivings that were so much a part of him, Calvin had to acknowledge that he did get some degree of pleasure from the new deference accorded to him by several of his so-called peers at Gadzooks. And, in some ways, even more of a kick from the impossible-to-disguise pique that so clearly and forthrightly oozed from others.

But hanging with Alonzo at lunch – and at times with both Alonzo and Joy after work – gave Calvin his first taste of belonging in his new environment. And that was doubly so when he accompanied the two of them to parts of LA he might otherwise never have known about, let alone visit.

If not certain of a future, at least Calvin seemed to be on a path toward an ever-increasing chance – one that owed not to wealth, influence, or lineage, but to ingenuity and resourcefulness – that he, far more than Mr. Oil Spill and the rest of those labeled by Beverly Steele *The sons and daughters of privilege* seemed to possess.

While not enough to make him starry-eyed, perky, or in any way a pollyanna, the change in his status was warmly welcomed. It made food taste better, sleep come more easily, the time spent at Gadzooks more manageable, and life itself more hopeful.

Never an Eagle Scout, Calvin, in true New Jersey fashion, could not quite manage to accept the change in fortune as a victory, or even as an end unto itself. Unable to resist the temptation to push his luck, his coffee breaks soon became a little longer – then a whole lot longer – which meant spending more and more time at Cash & Carry instead of hour after relentless hour in the Mail Room, plus occasionally popping into the Media Room to check in on Violeta.

Then, despite company policy that frowned on music from any external source, Calvin made his first foray into filling his work space with tunes of his choosing by playing a cut by Sharon Jones & the Dap-Kings, which he expected to follow in the days ahead by also featuring Ike & Tina, Howlin' Wolf, and even Screamin' Jay Hawkins.

The more he could get away with, the more Calvin found himself inclined to push. That soon came to mean worrying less and less about arriving at the designated hour. And, he decided, if the spirit moved him, it would soon also mean checking out from work early.

But despite the new liberties he was taking, never could Calvin fully ignore the awareness that Friday was looming. That, he never failed to recognized, mattered significantly, because weekends had become the passkey to his ever-improving niche at Gadzooks.

Not surprisingly, therefore, Thursday morning signaled the return of what he came to think of as the willies. Worse, Thursday night meant yet another round of list-making in the vain hope of ultimately falling asleep.

At 10:45 on Friday morning, a familiar-looking Lincoln Town Car headed south on La Cienega, then turned right onto Venice Boulevard.

With an undeniable case of the jitters, Calvin took in the old Helms Bakery and other sights in Culver City, then leaned forward after crossing the 405 Freeway and reaching Mar Vista.

"Mind pulling over?" he asked the same driver, Jose, as they reached a street called Grandview.

"Something wrong?" Jose replied as he steered the car into a space in front of the bowling alley on the northeast corner.

"Anything but," Calvin said, getting out of the car.

To Jose's dismay, Calvin crossed the street westbound, then did so southbound so as to check out a mural that featured, among other sights, Gaslight Anthem, the band he considered to be New Jersey's best since Southside Johnny & the Asbury Jukes. Then, crossing back, he realized that there was yet another must-see mural on the Grandview side of the bowling alley.

Calvin spent a couple of minutes taking in all the details of the scene that evoked the 1950's in a colorful way, then climbed into the back seat of the Lincoln.

"Like that kind of stuff?" Jose asked.

"Love it," replied Calvin, feeling considerably better.

"Then I should take you down to Venice some time, where the same guy painted a scene from a movie Orson Welles made, using a street with arches as a stand-in for Tijuana."

"*Touch Of Evil*," Calvin said.

"There you go. If I remember correctly, the mural's called *Touch Of Venice*."

"Sounds good to me."

"So you ready?"

"For the mural, or for where we really have to go?"

"Your call," said Jose.

With duty having superseded pleasure, the Lincoln turned

onto a quiet residential street a few minutes later, then pulled up in front of a lilac-colored stucco house with a white picket fence.

Judging from the meticulous flower beds, plus the elves scattered here and there around the front yard, Calvin immediately assumed that it was the dwelling of someone staid and conservative. So he was stunned, after walking up and ringing the bell, when the door opened and he found himself face-to-face with an incredibly buxom brunette in her early thirties who was literally bursting out of her skimpy, shocking pink blouse.

Gaping at cleavage the likes of which he had never before seen or imagined, Calvin was shaken from his ogling by a chuckle from someone clearly accustomed to such reactions.

"Like what you see, honey?" the woman asked.

"Umm... uhh..." was all a flustered Calvin could mumble.

"As I'm sure you've gathered," the woman said good-naturedly, "I'm Dusty."

"C-Calvin –"

"Tell you what, sweetie. Why don't you grab the suitcase and the garment bag? I'll take the little pink bag."

"You sure?" Calvin asked.

Dusty's only response was a wink.

Standing beside the open trunk of the Lincoln, Jose the driver caught sight of Dusty's monumental endowments, then gave Calvin a surreptitious nod of approval.

Then off they went toward the airport, with Calvin once again having made zero effort whatsoever to let Jose in on the fact that Dusty was in no way his date.

Despite the hustle and bustle at the airport, all activity seemed to come to a stop when out from the Lincoln Town Car stepped a most conspicuous figure: Dusty.

Never one to shy away from attention, Dusty happily smiled and waved at the mixture of admirers and gawkers. Then, with Calvin at her side, she strolled jauntily toward the entrance of the Southwest Terminal.

At the Security Checkpoint, having taken off their shoes, the two travelers put their carry-on luggage on the conveyor leading to the X-Ray inspection, then waited for their opportunity to pass through the metal detector.

But just as it was finally Dusty's turn to step through, a heavyset security guard with a name tag that said *SANCHEZ* picked up the small, shocking pink carrying case that she had insisted on toting herself.

"Mind if I open this?" the guard asked.

"Anything you want, honey," Dusty replied.

The security guard opened the case and started pulling out different objects, only to turn bright red with embarrassment at the realization that what he was holding were the items Dusty might have referred to as her toys: a collection of vibrators, dildos, feathers, masks, restraints, and other paraphernalia that, not surprisingly, also caught Calvin's eye.

Stunned, the security guard looked much more closely at the woman in front of him, leading to what Calvin took to be a spark of recognition.

"You're Dusty!" the guard bellowed as the realization hit home.

"Yes, and I've got something for you," Dusty quickly announced.

Foraging through the bag, she found a large manila envelope, then pulled out a glossy 8x12 photo and a pen. "What's your name, big boy?"

"Carlos."

Dusty autographed the photo with a flourish and handed it to the the guard, then kissed him on the cheek.

"Check out my website when you get a moment," she told him. "There's lots that's new and that I'm sure you'll like."

Then off toward the gate, she led Calvin.

Thanks to priority seating, Dusty and Calvin were among the first passengers to board the plane. Calvin hoisted their carry-on luggage into the bins overhead, then the two of them settled into seats.

"So," said Dusty a moment later, "I guess you now know what I do for a living. Embarrassed?"

"Not really?"

"Or troubled, since we'll be roommates?"

"No."

"Then go ahead and ask."

"Ask what?"

"That question I see lurking inside your devilish little mind."

"Well –" said Calvin awkwardly.

"Well, what?"

"How exactly did you –?"

When Calvin hesitated, Dusty finished his question. "Choose this line of work? Or hook up with George Kim?"

"Actually, both."

As other passengers started squeezing into neighboring seats, Dusty smiled.

"We'll talk about it all later," she promised.

While the plane made its way eastward, Calvin found himself wondering how the people back east – not just Ralphie and Plotkin, but a crowd that ranged from his old high school basketball teammates, to the crew who hung day and night at the pool hall, and even to his fellow record geeks who were scattered among various New York, New Jersey, and Connecticut towns – would respond if they knew what he was doing, and more importantly with whom.

That kind of speculation led to ruminations about what Calvin had come to think of as his *double life*. From the time he was growing up, he had consciously cast himself as a guy's guy – a jock who was often in trouble in school, ran with what was considered to be the wrong crowd, had minor brushes with the law, and was seemingly headed nowhere fast. It was an identity that he enjoyed, but it was equally, he came to realize, a form of protective coloration.

Yet there was also another side of him, one that sensed

that there was more to life than what he found either in his parents' house or in the street.   Music was his first secret pleasure, yet it was not one he could share with his contemporaries, whose tastes, even as a kid, had little overlap with his. Even more clandestine was his ever-growing love of books. Initially there were the ones he read because they were rumored to be dirty: "Candy," then "Naked Lunch," then best of all "Lolita."   The pleasure he derived from reading inevitably led him to the Beats: Kerouac, Ginsberg, Gregory Corso, Gary Snyder.   Then came other writers: Hemingway, Fitzgerald, and ultimately new favorites like James Salter, Frederic Raphael, Camus, and Pynchon. Yet for all sorts of reasons Calvin largely remained, even when he got to college, mainly what he called a closet reader.

The arts, in the world in which he was raised, were not merely nonexistent. They were frowned upon, thought to be suspicious, and dismissed as subversive – or worse, sissified.

The trips Calvin started making to New York were therefore largely on the sly. But, given his lack of funds, they also served as the inspiration for a kind of ingenuity that Calvin considered to be quintessentially Jersey. In addition to the part-time and summer jobs of his youth – mowing lawns, shoveling snow, working as a stock boy in a warehouse, and driving a truck after he got his license – every Saturday afternoon from the time he turned sixteen on, Calvin and a black football player friend would mix up a potpourri of sorts composed of twigs, leaves, catnip, and oregano, which would then be divided into small plastic bags. Early in the evening, the two buddies would cross the river and drift into Greenwich Village, where they would sell their goods to unsuspecting groups of kids from Westchester and Scarsdale who were in some ways precursors, only not quite so connected or lustrous, to his fellow interns at Gadzooks.

It was Calvin's introduction in the realm he started referring to as *mind over matter*, since instead of being pissed at being duped, the buyers would often rave about what they called "Dynamite shit," then later in the evening stop them so as to plead for more. On top of that, there was the additional kick that came from knowing that if ever the putative dealers got busted, there would be no grounds whatsoever for prosecution, since what he and his friend Bixie were selling was a harmless amalgam containing nothing even remotely narcotic or banned. But most important for Calvin was that in addition to paying for pizza and beer for the two young entrepreneurs – which they could buy, even while still underage, thanks to phony ID's – the evenings in New York also subsidized Calvin's purchases of books and records, plus his new-found interest in foreign films.

Seemingly lost in a voyage through the *Hows* and *Whys* of his earlier life, Calvin found himself shaken from his trip down memory lane while the plane flew over Arizona when Dusty suddenly tapped him on the shoulder.

"Hungry, sweetie?" she asked.

"A little bit."

"Well then I hope you like Indian food, 'cause guess who's got a couple of samosas."

Another Lincoln Town Car greeted the travelers at the Nashville airport, taking them, at Calvin's request, on a quick tour of Music City's foremost sights. In addition to the incredible array of churches that gave the town two religious nicknames – *The City Of Steeples* and *The Buckle Of The Bible Belt* – they made stops at several spots Calvin had researched on the internet. First came the Ryman Auditorium, known as The Mother Church of Country Music, which for many years housed the Grand Ole Opry. Then the Country Music Hall of Fame. And finally the street celebrated far and wide as Music Row, where singers as diverse as Roy Orbison, Eddy Arnold, Dolly Parton, and Waylon Jennings did significant recording. There, Calvin and Dusty got out of the car so as to take a peek at RCA Victor Studio B, where Elvis was reported to have cut over two hundred tracks.

Then it was off to the Hermitage Hotel, where bellhops swung into action as the Lincoln Town Car approached.

No longer a neophyte, Calvin strode confidently into the lobby, then up toward the front desk with far greater aplomb than in Seattle.

"Calvin Sands," he announced to the desk clerk, who couldn't help but gape at Dusty.

"From Gadzooks," replied the clerk.

"Absolutely."

"Then please let us welcome the two of you to Nashville," said the clerk with a smile.

A few minutes later, into a well-appointed hotel room stepped a bellhop, who turned on the lights, then carried in luggage as Calvin and Dusty followed.

Calvin tipped the bellhop, then turned to Dusty once they were alone.

"Hungry?" Calvin asked.

"Me? When am I not? Let me brush my hair, then we'll go get us some grub. Think there's Indian food around?"

"I kind of think we'll do better with barbecue, hush puppies, or fried chicken."

Dusty opened her purse and foraged unsuccessfully, then faced Calvin with a frown. "Mind waiting while I run down to the gift shop? Miss Genius here seems to have forgotten her brush."

"I'll go."

"You sure?"

"You wash up, and I'll be right back."

Dusty promptly thanked Calvin with a kiss on the cheek.

Stepping out of the elevator into the lobby just a couple of minutes later, Calvin immediately spotted a recognizable figure approaching: George Kim, accompanied by a pretty Korean-American woman wearing a wedding ring.

Calvin started to turn away, but not quickly enough, for an authoritative voice rang out.

"Calvin!" yelled George Kim.

Feigning surprise, Calvin turned in his direction. "How are

you?" he muttered.

"Say hello to my wife Ruby," Kim said. "This is Calvin, the bright young man I told you about."

With a smile, Ruby immediately extended a hand. "Thanks so much for helping carry the load," she said.

"Just doing what I can."

"Excuse us for a moment, will you, dear?" Kim said to his wife before walking Calvin several feet away. "There's a guy named Krause from a German firm called Vodaphone," he then told Calvin. "Word is he's leaning toward the competition, so I want you to move in on him."

Calvin nodded.

"Nailing him would be big for me," Kim continued. "And, just to be clear, for you, too."

Again Calvin nodded.

"Otherwise, things okay?" Kim asked.

Yet a third nod from Calvin yielded a chuckle from Kim. "Somebody's not exactly long-winded, huh?" the executive said. "Seems to me that Dusty might have taken your breath away."

Calvin made no effort to respond.

Dusty was seated on the hotel room floor in a full lotus position when in stepped Calvin, looking discernibly less chipper than when he left a short while earlier.

"You cool?" Dusty asked.

Faking it, Calvin nodded, which did little to fool Dusty.

"No, you're certainly not," she stated. "Let me guess, okay? Something tells me you bumped into Georgie-Porgie."

Calvin failed to reply, which did little to deter Dusty.

"And I bet," she said, "that little twerp wants you to do something shitty."

Calvin's only response was a shrug.

"Listen, kiddo," Dusty continued. "People think that what I do is simply about my bod. But the truth is, my business is 95% psychology. So don't for a moment think you can hide anything from me. Okay? If we're going to be roommates, one thing we're going to be is honest. Deal?"

Calvin considered Dusty's words for a moment, then smiled. "Deal."

"Perfect. Then how about you do a little searching on the internet? Mind doing that?"

"What exactly am I looking for?"

"A French restaurant where the two of us can charge a nice festive Champagne dinner to that little wienie – and do some serious talking while we're feasting. Sound good?"

"*Oui*," Calvin said, showing off his vast command of French.

9 PM found Calvin and Dusty seated in a quiet booth at a restaurant that was a strange amalgam of two disparate cultures – Music City and St. Germain-des-Pres – while a sommelier poured Veuve Clicquot into two flutes.

Dusty gave her approval with a smile. Then, as the sommelier left them, she raised her glass to toast.

"To indulgence?" she asked.

"No argument from me," Calvin replied.

The two of them took sips, which led to a smile on Dusty's face.

"Those hip-hop guys can keep their Cristal, not that it's so awful or anything," she said. "But I'll take Veuve Cliquot, Dom Perignon, or Laurent-Perrier any day. Keep that in mind for future reference, since I'm sure bubbly is always ever present on your mind."

"Day and night," Calvin responded playfully.

"So let me give you a little dose of what I refer to as Dusty's Philosophy. Everything in life, kiddo, is in one way or another a transaction. Sex, marriage, friendship, work – at some point or other it all comes down to the bottom line. Hope this doesn't come as too much of a shock."

"C'mon –"

"So if shit-for-brains wants you to do something, what you've got to do is figure out how to make sure the home team scores. Which, as I'm sure you gather, means you. With me?"

Calvin nodded, then Dusty took another sip of

Champagne.

"I'm not saying burn his ass, or stiff the company," she continued a moment later. "Except, maybe, for another bottle of the good stuff if the spirit moves us. But while getting him – and them – what they want, there's no reason in the world for you not to benefit as well. Bottom line? You score big? They do, too. Right?"

"Whatever you say."

"Well, what I say is let's order. Ever tried caviar? I mean, the real thing?"

"Not that I can remember."

"Well then, trust me, honey – you'd remember. If you and I can't have Indian food, guess who's going to score in a tasty and infinitely more extravagant way."

Pleasantly sated, and also somewhat tipsy, Calvin and Dusty entered the hotel room a couple of hours later with the intimacy of co-conspirators.

"Ask a question?" Calvin said as he kicked off his shoes.

"Fire away."

"If, as you were saying, life's a transaction –"

"Yeah?"

"How come you're here?"

"Certainly not because of Georgie-pooh," Dusty assured him. "See, I've got this whole Dusty line – not just DVDs, Blu-Rays, and signed photos, but assorted products, too."

"Should I ask what kind?"

"Not if it'll make you blush. And this is the kind of place where sales are strongest."

"The City of Steeples?"

"Kiddo, you bet. Over fifty percent of my sales come from the Bible Belt. So I'm here in this realm of the repressed to do some serious business. And the same, as I told you, should be true of you. Now, if you'll excuse me, this tired little Champagne fiend is about to get ready for beddie-bye."

With that, Dusty reached into her suitcase and grabbed a rather sheer negligee.

Twenty minutes later, with the lights out, the bedroom was illuminated only by the moon, plus colorful hints of neon from the street below.

In bed once again beside an extremely desirable female, Calvin found himself failing in his attempt to fall asleep. Wishing there were some way to will himself into dreamland, he was surprised to hear a voice beside him.

"You okay?" Dusty whispered.

"I guess."

"With all your non-stop tossing and turning, would it help for you to bounce on my bones?"

"What?" Calvin asked.

"Baby, it's not like you'd be the first. We can even call it professional courtesy."

Calvin sat up and looked at Dusty, who then sat up as well.

"You're really nice," Calvin said.

"And so are you. So?"

"I'd love to –"

"But?"

"Something tells me it'll be easier if we just stay friends."

To Dusty's dismay, Calvin proceeded to climb out of bed.

"Where you going?" Dusty asked.

"To run five miles or so," Calvin replied, searching for his running shoes.

The next morning, people galore were milling around the Registration tables when Calvin approached a young staffer with a name tag that read *LUANN*.

"Calvin Sands from Gadzooks," he announced.

"Welcome, Mr. Sands," she replied, pulling out a packet that included a name tag on a string that she placed around Calvin's neck.

"So tell me," he said, "any chance you'd know whether a guy named Gunther Krause from Vodaphone has checked in?"

Luann pointed to a tall, distinguished looking man in a gray suit who was sipping coffee.

"That's him right over there," she said merrily.

Thanking her, Calvin took a deep breath for confidence, then approached the German.

"Mr. Krause, I'm from Gadzooks."

Krause eyed Calvin with more than a measure of suspicion.

"You're not Mr. Kim," he stated.

"And you've got a keen eye for detail. My name is Calvin Sands, and, surprise, surprise, I'd like a shot at winning your account."

"You and fifty other people. Now if you'll excuse me —"

"Then I have to warn you —"

"About what?"

"That I'm very persistent," Calvin stated.

Despite Calvin's bravado, the day proved to be long, dull, and incredibly non-productive, with the speeches incredibly boring, the chicken served at lunch tasteless, the other participants dreary, and Gunther Krause willfully, obnoxiously, relentlessly off-putting.

When the day's formal activities ended, choosing to escape rather than to join others for a drink in the bar, Calvin trudged in defeat toward the hotel elevators.

By the time he got to the hotel room, Dusty, who had only just finished taking a shower, stepped out of the bathroom in a robe and instantly saw his gloom.

"What's wrong?" she asked.

Instead of answering, Calvin merely shrugged.

"Okay, let me guess," Dusty went on. "You got kidnapped by lesbian bikers."

Calvin shook his head.

"In a moment of despair, you joined the Marines?"

Another shake from Calvin.

"Then I'll bet it must have something to do with the guy that Georgie-Porgy wanted you to land."

Unhappily, Calvin acknowledged that it was so.

"So this douche bag," Dusty continued. "Where exactly is

he from?"

"Germany."

"Great!"

"What's so great about that?"

"Remember how I told you the Bible Belt is #1 when it comes to sales of my line of wares?"

Again Calvin acknowledged that she was correct.

"Well, Germany's #2 when it comes to perverts. What's this no-good character's name?"

"Why?"

"Because guess who's about to give him a call."

"You're crazy."

"That's a whole separate matter. But when it comes to human nature, remember, Dr. Freud had nothing on me."

"His name's Krause."

"Irving Krause?"

"Gunther."

To Calvin's astonishment, Dusty reached for the hotel phone.

"This'll never work," Calvin cautioned.

"Watch."

With utmost confidence, Dusty dialed the Operator, then spoke after being greeted. "Gunther Krause, please —"

Dusty winked at Calvin as she waited, then put on her sweetest, most seductive tone when she heard a male voice at the other end.

"Gunther Krause...? Then this is your lucky day. Does the name Dusty mean anything...? Yes, honey, that Dusty."

Proudly, Dusty flashed Calvin a thumbs-up.

Twenty minutes later, seated in a corner booth in the Hermitage bar, Gunther Krause's eyes lit up at the sight of Dusty approaching, his haughtiness and arrogance having miraculously given way to astonishment and awe.

"What an absolute pleasure!" Krause exclaimed as he got to his feet. "Please sit."

But when he saw Calvin walk in a moment later, in what

he quickly grasped was a carefully orchestrated delayed entrance, the German's jaw dropped.

Before Krause could question what was happening, Dusty reached into her handbag.

"I brought something for you," Dusty said as she pulled out a DVD titled, Calvin noted with amusement, "Night Of The Vibrator."

"*Danke schon!*" Krause gushed as she handed it to him.

"But that's not all," Dusty added provocatively.

While Calvin took a seat beside Dusty, she pulled out from her purse a see-through thong and a pen.

"Shall I sign it *To Gunther?*" she asked.

"Dare I ask first what all this is about?"

"As I told my dear friend Calvin, whom I believe you met this morning –"

"Yes."

"Everything in life's a transaction."

Calvin watched as Krause pondered that thought, then nodded knowingly.

"*To Gunther* would be perfect," the German said.

Stepping into the elevator, two drinks later, Calvin waited until the door closed, then faced Dusty.

"Not that I'm unhappy or anything, but can I ask why?" he asked.

"Really?"

"Yes, really."

"Because you're nice to me."

"C'mon –"

"I'm serious.

"And so am I," Dusty asserted. "In a dog-eat-dog world, where everybody and his uncle has got an angle, or an ulterior motive, or is simply trying to take advantage in some way or other, from the moment we met you've treated me like a person – not just a boob with boobs."

Week Four

BRIGHT AND EARLY Monday morning, while the usual cavalcade of expensive cars drove into the garage, George Kim, who was waiting nearby, extended a hand when out stepped Calvin.

"There's the man I want to see!"

The two of them shook, then Kim put an arm around Calvin.

"About what happened this weekend, that's our secret, right?" he said.

"Dusty who?" Calvin replied, bringing a smile to Kim's face.

"Atta boy! But the German guy, too."

"Whatever you say," Calvin said as he allowed Kim to lead him toward the building's entrance.

Along with several other people who had just arrived for work, George Kim and Calvin entered the Gadzooks offices a few minutes later only to be surprised by the sight of none other than Gunther Krause, who was standing near the reception desk.

"Gunther!" Kim exclaimed. "What in hell brings you here?"

"A quick stop-over on my way to Hong Kong," Krause answered. "Now if you'll excuse me, here's the man I wish to see."

Krause promptly pushed past Kim and warmly extended a hand to Calvin.

"Let me buy you some coffee," Krause said.

Take-out coffee in hand, Wesley Phillips was leaving Cash & Carry when Calvin stepped in together with Gunther Krause.

Aware that something seemed to be up, Wesley Phillips

eyed the men, then headed out the door.

Calvin, meanwhile, led the German up toward the counter, where Carrie smiled approvingly.

"I hear somebody's moving up the food chain," she said to Calvin.

"I don't know about that."

"Well, I do. So what'll it be, gentlemen?"

Calvin turned toward Krause, who was busy admiring Carrie's unmistakable good looks and bubbly cool.

"A double latte, please," Krause requested.

"And a green tea for me," added Calvin.

Forty-five minutes later, a clearly distressed Violeta trudged down the hall and pushed the button for the elevator, then was surprised when the door opened and out stepped Calvin, who instantly took stock of the state she was in.

"What's wrong?" he asked.

"Look to your left, look to your right," Violeta explained painfully.

"Shit! Anything I can do?"

"You bet," Violeta said. "Look after yourself."

Fighting tears, Violeta entered the elevator. Calvin watched the door close. Then, with an awareness that a legitimate sword of Damocles had finally replaced mere threats, he girded himself for whatever might lie ahead.

Only after a couple of deep breaths did he finally stride toward the Gadzook offices.

The moment Calvin opened the door, Robert Williams, who was standing at the reception desk, turned on him with thinly veiled jealousy.

"They're waiting for you in H.R.," Robert hissed.

"Who in Human Resources?"

"The Steel Maiden herself," Robert informed him.

A harried-looking assistant with a name plate that read *ANDREW* glanced up from his computer when the door to

Human Resources swung open.

"Calvin Sands," Calvin announced as he entered.

Not long on personality, Andrew promptly reached for the phone.

"That intern you wanted," he said.

Moments later, Beverly Steele made no effort to get up from behind her desk when Calvin stepped into her office.

"Please close the door," she said, which Calvin did. Then she waved him to a seat.

"You're making quite a name for yourself," Beverly stated after an elongated moment in which she studied him silently.

"I'm trying."

"And, it seems, carving quite a niche."

"Does that bother you?"

"Actually," Beverly said with a chuckle, "I'm getting quite a kick out of it. I love seeing the anointed squirm. But –"

"But what?"

"Know much about scuba diving?"

"Why?"

"The first lesson they teach you is about not making too rapid an ascent. Know why?"

"Why?"

"Because too rapid an ascent can be fatal."

Instead of wincing, Calvin merely smiled. "Is that all?" he asked.

"Hardly. You're out of the mail room."

"I-I'm fired?"

"Not exactly," Beverly replied.

At just that very moment, the door swung open.

"So is this the guy?" Steve Norris, still scruffy, wearing flip-flops, and seeming like the very personification of cool, asked as he entered Beverly's office.

When Beverly nodded, Norris turned toward Calvin and extended a hand.

"Steve Norris," he said.

Ambling down the hall, Jonathan Olson, Samantha Steinberg, and Robert Williams did a group double-take at the sight of Steve Norris approaching with an arm around Calvin.

Steve Norris paid zero attention to the three of them as, to their collective dismay, he led Calvin toward an unoccupied office, where he stopped and pointed inside.

"A little bit more comfy than the Mail Room?" Norris asked.

"You bet."

To everyone's surprise, Norris suddenly turned toward the interns who were watching, then pointed at Mr. Oil Spill.

"You are –?"

"Jonathan Olson, sir."

"Tell Maintenance they've got exactly ten minutes to get this man's name on the door."

While Jonathan Olson seethed, Samantha Steinberg and Robert Williams watched with a mixture of astonishment, bewilderment, and envy as Steve Norris led Calvin down the hall.

Thanks to the lull between breakfast and lunch, Cash & Carrie was relatively subdued when Calvin stepped in.

Not seeing Carrie, he approached May.

"Carrie here?" he asked.

"One minute," May replied.

Calvin watched May walk toward the back of the restaurant, where she opened the back door and popped her head through, then called out something in Mandarin.

A moment later, Carrie appeared.

"Mr. Fast Track," she said at the sight of Calvin.

"I wouldn't go that far."

"So what can I do you for?"

"How about coming with me to the Dodger game?"

"Tonight?"

Calvin nodded. "I've got two great seats, and we don't even have to call it a date."

"I'd like to –"

"Really?"

"But —"

"Yeah?"

"There's someplace I have to be."

"Oh," said Calvin, instantly deflated.

"You see, I design jewelry —"

Studying the look on Calvin's face, Carrie grimaced.

"You don't believe me," she said.

"What do you mean?"

"About having to be somewhere."

Calvin merely shrugged.

"You want proof?" Carrie asked.

"What if I say yes?"

"Then come with me."

Early that evening, at the wheel of a Honda Civic Hybrid fighting its way east across town, Carrie turned to Calvin in the passenger seat.

"I can't believe you actually passed up the game," she said.

"Maybe I prefer being with you."

"Proof that you're crazy. What if I tell you I bring bad luck?"

"C'mon —"

"And have this crazy fascination with daytime soaps —"

"Which I doubt —"

"And secretly listen to Justin Bieber and Lady Gaga —"

"Ouch —"

"And am president of the local chapter of the NRA —"

"Really want to get rid of me?" Calvin asked.

"Maybe —"

"Then you'll have to do better than that."

"Okay, but keep this in mind —"

"What?"

"You can't say I didn't warn you," Carrie affirmed before pointing to a bag in the back seat. "If you're hungry, there's some Shandong beef rolls."

Not quite an hour later, the two of them arrived at a hangar-like space in Silverlake that had been transformed into an evening swap meet for artists and artisans, whose wares were being set up for sale by painters, sculptors, and designers.

Toting leather bags filled with Carrie's work, they weaved their way toward their destination, while Carrie, clearly a regular in the environment, made a point of smiling at some people, waving to others, as well as hugging and kissing a few that they passed.

Upon reaching the space they sought, Calvin watched as Carrie opened the bags and readied her displays of rings, bracelets, and necklaces, most of which featured imaginative combinations of brightly colored stones.

"Really fine work," Calvin said once everything was set up.

"Spoken as a connoisseur?"

"Spoken as someone who knows absolutely nothing whatsoever about jewelry, but likes what he sees."

"That's sweet," said Carrie warmly. "With this crazy economy, let's hope there are some customers who feel the same."

Barely three hours later, out into the parking lot came Calvin and Carrie, who loaded the bags of jewelry into the trunk, then climbed back into the Honda Civic.

Settling behind the wheel, Carrie faced Calvin.

"So," she said, "the single most boring night of your life?"

"I loved it."

"C'mon –"

"Okay, so I loved being with you. Mind if I ask a question?"

"Shoot."

"How'd someone who's obviously so talented –"

"Wind up running a breakfast-and-lunch place?" Carrie asked, finishing Calvin's question. "It was my Dad's. But then he got sick, and –"

"You came to the rescue?"

Carrie nodded. "How about you?" she asked. "What's

your Dad do?"

"Mostly sits around and mopes."

"Seriously?"

"His job got outsourced to some third world country, and he hasn't found anything other than part-time stuff since. But let's talk about you. I mean you're really good."

"But not exactly a household name."

"Yet."

"One of us is optimistic as well as sweet. Which is why I want to give you this."

To Calvin's surprise, Carrie handed him a bracelet.

"You don't have to."

"And if I want to?"

"Thanks.

Calvin proudly put the bracelet on his left wrist.

"Now," he said, "can I buy you a pizza in return?"

"I'm not really hungry."

"Then how about just a dessert?"

"It's been a long day."

"Hey, a hot fudge sundae? A glass of wine? Some herb tea? There's a place I know of that's close to where you live."

Taken aback, Carrie eyed Calvin strangely.

"Wait a second," she said. "How do you know where I live?"

"With my new position, I have access to everyone with a Gadzooks account – which means I know everything about you."

"Everything?"

"Well, almost."

"You are certainly persistent."

"Determined," Calvin said, correcting her.

Carrie studied Calvin for a moment, then took a breath.

"Let me be honest with you –" she said before hesitating.

Darkening, Calvin finished her thought. "You promised to meet somebody."

Seeing the change in Calvin, Carrie admitted the truth sheepishly.

"Will you take a rain check?" she asked.

Clearly hurt, Calvin opened the passenger door.

"At least let me give you a ride," Carrie said.

"I'll manage," were Calvin's parting words as he climbed out of the car.

Instead of going to a gun shop or finding a bridge from which to jump, Calvin did something that he knew to be almost equally idiotic: he decided to hitchhike.

The result was that for fifteen minutes he was ignored, laughed at, taunted, and given the finger until, to his surprise, an Edsel, of all things, pulled over.

At the wheel, it turned out, was a guy pushing seventy with whatever vestiges were left of his gray hair pulled back in a pony tail. "You must be either crazy or pissed off," the guy said.

"Both," Calvin replied.

"So where you headed?"

"Santa Monica."

"Where once upon a time I saw great acts at the Santa Monica Civic. Hop in."

With Love's "Forever Changes" album playing on the Edsel's stereo system, the two of them headed west, while the guy, who introduced himself as Bill the Barbarian, a former bouncer at rock clubs, regaled Calvin with stories of hitchers he picked up back before the world got, as he put it, scary and violent. There was Larry "Wild Man" Fischer, the schizophrenic later known as the Godfather Of Outsider Music, who used to sing songs, including "Merry-Go-Round," for a dime on the street. There was Nico, the once-upon-a-time singer with the Velvet Underground, whose carrying case overflowed with a dazzling array of pharmaceuticals. Then there was Billy Preston, who on a drizzly night was not quite able to remember where he had parked the Rolls that he purchased with the royalties from "Will It Go Round In Circles" and "You Are So Beautiful." Plus, of course, groupies, runaways, and even, on a night not to be forgotten, a member of the Manson family.

By the time the Edsel pulled up in front of Gadzooks, in addition to being filled with all sorts of unexpected LA lore, Calvin was also feeling infinitely better.

"Here's something for you," Calvin said, taking the bracelet given to him by Carrie off his wrist and handing it to the driver.

"You sure?"

"Positive," Calvin said as Bill the Barbarian happily placed it on his wrist.

After watching the Edsel pull away, rather than call it quits on the evening, Calvin retrieved his car, then jumped onto the 10 Freeway.

It was to Crenshaw Boulevard that he headed, then south to a black cultural mecca called Leimert Park, where not another white person was in sight when the dented VW pulled into a space on Degnan Boulevard.

To the surprise of the brothers hanging on the street, Calvin climbed out of his car, then strolled toward a storefront called the World Stage, from which upbeat sounds could be heard.

In a cozy venue dedicated to spoken word in the early evening, then jazz thereafter, a bunch of night owls, surrounded by huge photos of Miles, Mingus, Monk, and other luminaries, were enjoying the band that was playing.

But for Calvin it was not just any old band, for leading the six-piece ensemble on flute was Joy Steward, while on drums was none other than Alonzo Stevens.

Receiving a knowing glance from Alonzo, Calvin took a seat and, as the set continued for four more songs, slowly but steadily allowed himself to let go of any remaining woes.

Once the set was over, out from the club stepped Alonzo and Calvin. A couple of tough-looking guys on the street were clearly surprised by the sight of a pale face in their 'hood, but they were quickly placated by a look from Alonzo, who then turned his attention to his protege-of-sorts.

"Seems like somebody's getting closer and closer with each passing day," he said.

"Except I don't get it," Calvin responded.

"Get what?"

"Norris is starting to hint about moving me into his guest house."

"And that's not better than your ratty motel?"

"But why?"

"Why what?"

"The weekend thing – being a beard – I get. But now suddenly a guest house?"

"Want the truth? If you're up for it, he'll probably even pay for tennis and sailing lessons."

"What in hell for?"

"So you can babysit the wife."

"Tell me you're kidding."

"Milk it, and who knows? One of these days maybe you'll even pass for one of those rich kids you love so much."

As Alonzo chuckled at his own joke, out from the World Stage came Joy, who kissed Calvin on the cheek.

"Thanks for coming out to hear us," she said.

"My pleasure. Your band's great."

Joy promptly tapped Alonzo on the shoulder.

"Your friend's got impeccable taste and judgment."

Carefully avoiding Cash & Carrie, and not wanting either the glares he got from certain interns or the brown-nosing he received from others, Calvin, when not at the park with Alonzo at lunch, spent much of the next couple of days focusing on assignments given to him by Steve Norris.

Mainly, that consisted of examining flow charts, then doing projections based on age, gender, and level of education.

While interesting to a degree, the extrapolations were neither particularly taxing nor extremely time consuming, which meant that Calvin, while doing his best to ignore the omnipresent and ever-mounting concern among the other interns as to who would be the next one to be sent packing, took to surfing the internet for long stretches in search of topics that intrigued him.

One morning was devoted largely to determining the greatest baseball players of all time who had not been inducted into the Hall of Fame at Cooperstown. Confirming his suspicions that racism, whether conscious or inadvertent, was at work, the vast majority of those overlooked – Minnie Minoso, Vic Power, Tony Oliva, Luis Tiant, Davy Concepcion, and Camilo Pascual – proved to be Latino, though Calvin did acknowledge that there was also a case to be made for palefaces like Bert Blyleven and Jim Kaat as well.

The next afternoon, even as he heard his contemporaries gossiping about the likely next victim, Calvin's search was for the most under-appreciated stars in the different arts. James Carr and Howard Tate were his nominees in Soul music, Clifford Brown, Bud Powell, and Art Blakey in jazz, the Velvet Underground, Mitch Ryder, and the Chambers Brothers in Rock & Roll, Georges Braque, Odilon Redon, and the Douanier Rousseau in painting, Francois Villon and Gregory Corso in poetry, Preston Sturges and Claude Sautet in filmmaking, and last but not least Jorge Semprun and Rabelais in fiction.

Much of yet another day was devoted to a quest for great quotes, especially those not often taught or heard in school. "A man is great by deeds, not by birth," attributed to someone named Chanakya, understandably hit a responsive chord deep within Calvin. Then there was one from a guy named Switzer, whom Calvin presumed was not the erstwhile football coach at Oklahoma: "It is better to remain silent at the risk of being thought a fool than to talk and remove all doubt." And a great line from Milton Berle also seemed appropriate: "If opportunity doesn't knock, then build a door." But his favorite by far was one from the economist John Stuart Mill, which he couldn't wait to use on his uncle Bert, a troglodyte who called anyone in favor of gun control a *candy-ass un-American libtard*: "Although it is not true that all conservatives are stupid people, it is true that most stupid people are conservative."

All the while Calvin found himself facing what grew into an almost unbearable kind of what he called "Waiting for the other shoe to drop." Having learned early in his life that, in the parlance of New Jersey pool halls, that *There ain't no such thing as a free lunch*, he waited for the expected demand for a *quid pro quo* from Steve Norris.

But Monday brought nothing. Tuesday, as T-Bone Walker sang in "Stormy Monday, was "just the same." And even Wednesday was surprisingly quiet and uneventful.

It wasn't until Thursday, with Calvin's new case of the heebie-jeebies reaching its peak, that Norris popped into his office for a chat.

"Comfy?" Norris asked after looking around the office, which was still quite bare.

"More or less," Calvin replied.

"Then let's up the more, and reduce the less. What kind of stuff would you like on the wall? Paintings? Posters? Photos? Think of a motif that suits you. We can go sports, art, music, or whatever. Sound good?"

"That's really nice."

"C'mon, nice is for chumps. What counts are vibe, image, mood – that kind of stuff. So what else do you need to know?"

"Not a whole lot."

"Okay, then let's talk turkey," Norris said. "You're probably wondering when I'm going to order you or impose upon you to do something for me. Right?"

"Not really."

"Which means, bet your sweet ass. Well, here's something you need to know about me. Unlike Donnelly or Kim, I don't function that way. I don't like to give an order or an ultimatum. Understood?"

Calvin nodded.

"So what I'm going to do instead of imposing or forcing is ask," Norris continued. "Any chance of enticing you, or appealing to your good nature, to do a solid for me this weekend?"

Pleased that the waiting game was over and that everything was finally out in the open, Calvin smiled.

"What are friends for?"

Though Thursday night brought another case of the jitters, the magnitude was nowhere near what it had been the two weeks before. The difference, Calvin understood, owed to experience, which resulted in his possessing a certain degree of confidence and composure.

Having weathered two contrasting situations, each of which had clearly made major contributions to his professional ascent, as well as to his life, Calvin felt entitled to take some comfort in the belief that there was little that could surprise him.

At 10 AM Friday a familiar-looking Lincoln Town Car drove east on Sunset until it reached Echo Park, then turned onto a residential street lined with low-rise apartment houses.

Reaching its destination, the car pulled over in front of a fire hydrant. Then out stepped Calvin, who walked dutifully toward the building.

A couple of moments later, having heard the bell ring, a young woman scurried to open the door of her second-floor apartment.

Only then did Calvin realize that his so-called date for the weekend was none other than fellow intern Amy Kawasaki.

"I-I didn't realize," uttered a stunned Amy.

"M-me, neither."

For a moment the two of them stood in silence until Amy let out a sigh.

"Welcome to the real world, huh?" she said softly.

"I guess."

"Well," Amy said with a shrug. "I suppose there's no reason to give up a trip to Miami."

Calvin made no attempt to argue.

Standing beside the Lincoln Town Car, Jose the driver gave Calvin yet another surreptitious wink at the sight of pretty Amy, then hoisted the luggage into the trunk. Then off the three of them went toward the airport, with conversation non-existent.

The flight, too, was singularly devoid of chit-chat, with both Calvin and Amy alternately feigning sleep or trying to immerse themselves in reading.

The result was an awkward, strained, seemingly endless journey which certainly did not bode well for the rest of the weekend.

Nor did matters improve while riding in the Lincoln Town Car that drove them to South Beach, where they gazed at the Art Deco palaces rather than at each other until they pulled up at an oceanfront hotel called the Canyon Ranch.

Still making no effort to converse, they were an anomaly amongst the smiling faces as they lumbered through the lobby to check in.

It was dark by the time the door to their hotel room was opened by a bellhop, who turned on the lights as he carried in their luggage.

Tip in hand, the bellhop then took off, leaving Amy and Calvin alone with the absurd reality of their situation.

"I still don't believe this," Amy said, assessing their predicament.

"That makes two of us," Calvin added.

"Well, at least we're talking."

"What does that mean?"

"We were both so freaked out we didn't say a word the entire flight."

"I did."

"When?"

"When I had to get up to pee. I said *Excuse me.*"

Amy eyed Calvin for a moment, then giggled. "Know

what's funny?" she asked.

"What?"

"Everybody had you pegged as one of the first to get bounced."

"Including you?"

Amy winced guiltily. "The crazy thing is, now you'll probably wind up running the whole damn company."

"What about you?"

Amy shrugged.

"What's that mean?" Calvin asked.

"I'm just doing the best I can," she said with a sigh. "Know what I need? I need to stretch my legs, breathe some real air, and clear out my head. Feel like joining me?"

"I'd love to," Calvin said without the slightest trace of irony.

Illuminated by a full moon overhead, the beach behind the Canyon Ranch Hotel looked almost magical as Calvin and Amy approached.

"Anybody special in your life?" Amy asked.

"Not exactly," Calvin replied sadly.

"Which means, if I read you correctly, you're game, but she's not 100% sure."

"I'd settle for even 10% sure."

"Feel like getting hammered?"

"I think my arm can be twisted."

"Ever have a mojito?"

"I had measles and mumps," Calvin said.

"Calvin —"

"Sorry, I'm a laugh whore."

"What do you say we start spending Gadzooks' money?"

Calvin did not protest.

Ten minutes later, into the Canyon Ranch bar stepped a guy wearing a pair of raggedy cut-offs and a vintage Hawaiian shirt as well as his customary flip-flops. It was none other than Steve Norris, accompanied by his striking German wife, and the two of them immediately noticed a two-fisted mojito carrier headed their way.

"Somebody's ready for action," Norris shouted to Calvin, who stopped in his tracks. "Calvin, say hello to my wife Petra."

"Nice to meet you," Petra said.

"You, too," Calvin replied.

Norris wasted no time in patting his wife's arm. "Forgive me for a moment, babes," he said to her before putting a hand on Calvin's shoulder and leading him toward the door to the lobby.

Once they were out of Petra's hearing distance, Norris faced Calvin, who was uncomfortable not only because of the two mojitos he was holding.

"Everything cool?" Norris asked.

Calvin nodded.

"Amy?" Norris continued. "And the conference tomorrow?"

Again Calvin nodded.

"But you're wondering why," Norris went on, "since I've already got filet mignon I'm trying to sneak a little sushi on the side. Right?"

"Not really," Calvin mumbled, trying his best to play it suave.

"Bullshit. And if I were you, I'd be wondering, too. Ready to hear why?"

"Sure."

"Because I can, Calvin," Norris stated. "Because I damn well fucking can. Now go and give the pretty lady her drink."

With that, Norris strode back toward the bar.

It wasn't a mojito or two that Calvin and Amy shared. Rather, it was mojito after mojito after mojito, followed by some Cuban chicken and platanos, then yet another couple of rounds of tasty rum-powered drinks.

Willfully, deliberately, forthrightly blitzed, the supposed couple finally staggered back to their room at an ungodly hour and immediately fell into bed, their drunkenness and slumber obviating any need Calvin might have otherwise felt for one of his late night jogs.

The next morning, when Calvin stepped out of the bathroom after a shower, he was surprised to find Amy, wearing only a bra and panties, standing on her head.

"You okay?" he asked.

"You know those guys with jackhammers who dig up the streets?"

"What about 'em?"

"Some of 'em crawled into my head while we were downing our fourth or fifth mojito. Calvin?"

"Uh-huh?"

"This trip, or whatever you want to call it –"

"Yeah?"

"It'll stay between us?"

"Whatever you say."

The meetings that day found Calvin present in body, but not in spirit. While nursing a hangover, he spent considerable time, when not dozing off, pondering Beverly Steele's warning about too rapid an ascent.

That led to an all-too-familiar kind of self doubt. *Who am I?* Calvin found himself wondering. And *What am I?* And above all, *What in hell am I supposed to do with my life?*

When no answers had materialized by the time evening rolled around, he once again threw caution to the wind by joining Amy for far too many mojitos.

Not surprisingly, their flight home on Sunday was spent recovering rather than chatting, with both of them too hung over to ponder what the week ahead might bring.

Week Five

MONDAY MORNING FOUND STEVE NORRIS standing with a coffee container in hand when out from the Gadzooks garage stepped Calvin.

"My main man!" Norris exclaimed. "Got places to go? People to see?"

"You tell me."

"How about you and I take a drive?"

East on the 10 Freeway came a bright red Porsche convertible with the top down, and Calvin, in the passenger seat, feeling as though he'd entered a parallel universe.

With the wind blowing his hair in every direction imaginable, and his adrenalin pumping, Calvin enjoyed the ever-increasing speed as Steve Norris weaved through traffic, then swung onto the 405 Northbound.

On they went until they reached Mulholland Drive, where Norris swung off the freeway. Then the fun really began.

Showing off both his driving skills and his car's maneuverability, Norris treated the celebrated windy road, which Calvin happily recognized from scores of films and TV shows, as though it were a key stop on the Grand Prix circuit.

Then finally they turned onto a long, curvy driveway that led to a spacious ranch house with a view of both Downtown LA and nearly the entire San Fernando Valley.

Climbing out of the passenger seat, Calvin could not help but go wide-eyed, not merely at the amazing views, but also at the pool and tennis court that were part of what seemed like a dream come true of a SoCal property.

Noting Calvin's reaction, Norris smiled. "You a tennis buff?" he asked.

"Far from it."

"That'll change once we get you lessons. Let me show you the guest house."

Norris led the way into the back yard, then up to a bungalow-style building.

Proudly, he opened the door so that Calvin could get a glimpse of the interior of a bright and tidy dwelling that was the opposite end of the spectrum from the oppressive motel room that had been serving as his temporary abode.

"Say the word," Norris announced, "and it's yours."

"In exchange for?"

Steve Norris chuckled.

"No beating around the bush, huh?" he said. "Then let's put our cards on the table. It's called *You scratch my back, I'll scratch yours*. With me?"

Calvin said nothing, so Norris continued.

"There's an old joke that describes the life I've settled into: *I married you for better or for worse, but not for lunch*. Petra's gorgeous, and wonderful in many ways – especially in what I call *quality time*."

"And the rest of the time?"

"That, my friend, is where you come in. Play tennis with her... Go with her to Thai cooking classes... Do the New York Times crosswords together..."

"While you get your playtime?"

Steve Norris wasted no time in copping to it. "Not particularly painful or onerous, as I see it."

"And what about work?"

"We'll figure all that out. But meanwhile, you'll live well, expand your horizons, and get to drive the little Beemer we keep as a spare. Trust me when I tell you that life can be far, far worse."

Having to race off to a meeting in Burbank, Steve Norris dropped Calvin off at the Gadzooks building, where he immediately bumped into Alonzo.

"Buy you a cup of tea?" Calvin asked.

"Love to, but I've got to run an errand."

"Before you do, can I ask a favor? There's an app I've been hearing about that's supposed to be spectacular in helping to avoid traffic jams –" Calvin began, only to be interrupted.

"And you, like most people, are having trouble getting it hooked up," Alonzo stated. "Which is why you want me to do for you."

"Bingo."

"Gotta warn you though. You're taking a chance."

"Because?"

"Twenty percent or so of the people wind up with heavy-duty headaches and problems."

"I've got good phone karma."

Alonzo took Calvin's cell and did some tinkering, then handed it back to him. "Here's hoping."

"What's the worst that can happen?" Calvin asked as Alonzo headed off on his errand.

Thanks to the much-appreciated lull between breakfast and lunch, Carrie was thumbing through a magazine in the restaurant bearing her name when Calvin, who had not made an appearance since the night he felt jilted, entered with a strange and somehow distant look on his face.

"Guess somebody's not quite as mad at me," Carrie said. Then, seeing the expression on his face, she added, "You okay?"

"Ever find yourself wondering who you are?" Calvin replied. "Or who you want to be?"

"Only every day of the week or so. Why?"

"A few months ago I was in New Jersey, trying to teach a bunch of rich kids who didn't give a shit about anything but a Porsche or a BMW –"

"And now?"

"I just drove in a Porsche, and somebody's trying to give me a Beemer."

Out from the kitchen stepped May, who smiled at Calvin, then started making herself a pot of Puer tea.

"Okay, joke of the day," said Carrie a moment later. "What's the difference between a porcupine and a Porsche?"

"I give up."

"With a porcupine, the pricks are on the outside. So tell me –"

"Yeah?"

"Like Indian food?"

"Why?"

"Because tonight I'd like to buy you dinner."

Suddenly Calvin felt better than he had in ages.

Twenty minutes later, out from Cash & Carrie stepped Calvin, who was totally wrapped up in thought as he headed toward the entrance to the Gadzooks building – until, that is, he was jostled from his reverie by a flying tackle!

Stunned, Calvin was in the process of fighting for his freedom when he suddenly realized that it was not a mugger, a terrorist, or a cop who had nailed him, but his homeboy from Jersey, Ralphie.

And approaching was the third *amigo*, Plotkin.

"Told you we'd be out here soon!" Plotkin exclaimed.

"Why didn't you call me?" Calvin asked.

"We tried you once we landed," Ralphie added.

"Sure your cell is working?" Plotkin asked.

Calvin pulled out his iPhone. But before he could check to see if it was working post-Alonzo's tinkering, Ralphie stopped him.

"Forget that and hit your office phone!" Ralphie insisted.

"And call Jasmine Simms!" Plotkin added.

"Tell her your boys are ready to meet her friends!" Ralphie emphasized.

With everything that was going on in his life, events at Gadzooks seemed somewhat less important that day, even when word went out that a pushy yet not particularly bright intern named Pat Stacy had been let go.

Though Calvin had still never stepped foot on one of SoCal's legendary beaches, it was to the ocean that he sent Ralphie and Plotkin, telling them to start in Malibu, then work their way south to the Santa Monica Pier before finishing the afternoon on Ocean Front Walk in Venice.

That gave Calvin some breathing room in which to contemplate and wrestle with the decisions he had to make.

But the respite came to an abrupt halt when the two temporary refugees from Jersey appeared toward the end of the afternoon.

"We're hijacking you!" Plotkin announced.

"Lead on for some brewskis!" Ralphie urged.

Too many beers, bar snacks, and silly jokes later, a voice rang out in a rented Dodge that was driving down Ocean Avenue in Santa Monica.

"What'dya mean you don't know her?" bellowed Plotkin, who was at the wheel. "That's pure and simple bullshit!"

"It was a weird thing that happened," Calvin tried to explain.

"Yeah, right!" said Plotkin.

"So what other chicks do you know?" Ralphie asked.

"Hardly any."

"Ralphie," said Plotkin, "somebody's holding out on us."

As Plotkin stopped for a red light, another car honked. With customary Jersey sophistication, Plotkin promptly gave the other driver the finger.

"Honk this, douche bag!" he shouted.

But to Plotkin's dismay, the other car honked again, then pulled up beside them. Instantly the three guys turned to see something – actually someone! – totally unexpected. For at the wheel of an Escalade, grinning from ear to ear, was none other than Daisy.

"Calvin, honey!" Dusty said in her unmistakable come-hither voice. "I miss you!"

Behind the wheel, Plotkin nearly had kittens.

"Y-you k-know Dusty?" he mumbled.

As though it was no big thing, Calvin nodded. Then he pointed toward a side street.

"Pull over," he instructed Plotkin, while waving to Dusty to do the same.

Both cars turned onto a street called Arizona, then came to a stop in a red zone.

Plotkin and Ralphie watched with amazement as Dusty and Calvin jumped out of their respective cars and hugged.

"I've been missing you, baby!" Dusty shouted.

"And I've been missing you!" Calvin added.

"So when are we finally going to make up for that Indian food we never got in Nashville?"

"Indian food!" Calvin bellowed.

Instantly, he turned on Plotkin.

"Gimme the keys!"

To the astonishment of the others, Calvin grabbed the keys from Plotkin and ran to the Dodge, then climbed behind the wheel and burned rubber.

Never one to fluster, Dusty turned toward Plotkin and Ralphie with a smile.

"You guys hungry?" she asked.

While trying to navigate the rented Dodge through the barrage of traffic on the landlocked Westside at rush hour, Calvin pulled out his iPhone and tried in vain to dial a number, only to remember Alonzo's warning, plus his friends' complaint about the phone not working.

Flinging the piece of useless technology onto the seat behind him, Calvin inched his way east through the impasse that was Ocean Park Boulevard, then finally turned onto Centinela southbound. Cursing as he crept along, Calvin at last reached Venice Boulevard, then had to wait what felt like forever until he got a chance to make a left.

Nearing Motor Avenue several minutes later, Calvin spotted a Nissan minivan that was about to back into that rarest of all things – a parking space – then did something dastardly by zooming in head first.

Though aware that he had earned the well-deserved fury of the other driver, who justifiably honked and shouted vociferously, Calvin nonetheless dashed toward an Indian restaurant called Mayura.

Inside the cozy restaurant, the diminutive owner, who was dressed in a colorful sari, looked up as in burst Calvin, who peered every which way to no avail.

"May I help you?" asked the woman in accented English.

"I'm looking for a really cute Chinese girl –"

"I'm afraid she left."

"Left?"

"But she did leave a message –"

"Okay –"

"But it's not very nice –"

"It's okay, I'm a big boy."

"She said –"

"Yes?"

"That you should kindly drop dead."

Calvin stared at the Indian woman for a moment, then stepped outside, let out a scream, and pounded his fist against the wall!

Not the least bit eager to face the world, Calvin spent the entire next day on a bender with Plotkin and Ralphie that took them to pubs, gin mills, and dive bars in every corner of LA. They hit Tom Bergin's on Fairfax, Cole's P&E downtown, the Burgundy Room in Hollywood, Bar Melody near the airport, and even JP's in Santa Monica, then finally collapsed back at Calvin's raunchy motel room.

The following morning, with the sun just beginning to peek through the ratty shades, Calvin started to step over Plotkin, who was snoring on the floor, when Ralphie, looking half-dead, stumbled out of the bathroom.

"You alive?" Ralphie asked.

"Just barely."

"That makes two of us. But Sleeping Beauty and I have a flight to catch."

Leaning over, Ralphie started to shake Plotkin, who tried to swat his hand away.

"I need sleep!" Plotkin protested.

"Not if you want to get on our plane," Ralphie responded.

As Plotkin groaned, Ralphie turned to Calvin. "Promise me something?" he asked.

"What's that?"

"You'll never leave LA. Where we're headed, it'll be 20 degrees in no time, and the girls all have mustaches. Which means, *amigo*, the two of us will be back."

By 8:30, people galore were grabbing lattes, muffins, bagels, and even dim sum at Cash & Carrie, which meant that Carrie was hardly at rest when Calvin, clearly the worse for wear, entered.

Exuding contrition, he waited on line until it was his turn, then faced Carrie.

"So what'll it be, stranger?" she asked.

"Aggravation over easy, plus a side of humble pie. Still pissed?"

"I was."

"And then?"

"A guy I stopped seeing called, so I guess everything worked out okay."

"Pow!" Calvin exclaimed.

"C'mon —"

"It's not like I'm gonna say *Oh goodie!*"

"You'll get over it."

A few minutes later, Matt Donnelly was approaching Cash & Carrie when out stepped Calvin, armed with a container of green tea plus an order of *har gow*.

"So how's China's gift to mankind?" Donnelly asked, pointing inside.

"Peachy," Calvin replied.

"You know, I finally figured out why it is she shoots us down."

"Oh yeah?"

"Lipstick lesbian."

"Bullshit."

"Then give me another explanation," Donnelly demanded.
"Intelligence."

At 10:45 that morning, Alonzo Stevens, who was walking
down the Gadzooks corridor, ignored a *What up?* from
Jonathan Olson, then poked his head into Calvin's new office.
"Lunch and b-ball?" Alonzo asked.
"Can't," Calvin said, looking up from his laptop. "It's
moving day."
"Norris came through?"
Calvin peered at Alonzo. "Is there anything you don't
know?"
"Yup, the secret to fame and fortune. Need any help?"
"With moving, or with life?"
"Hey, you're the one who wanted the fast track."
"Doesn't mean it's not complicated."
"Want the truth?" Alonzo asked.
"Sure."
"Life is complicated."

In somewhat of a state of shock, Calvin spent lunchtime
moving his minimal belongings from the war zone of Motel
Hell to an area that his Jersey friends would consider to be a
step or two above paradise.
Still unable to believe that he was moving up in the world,
both literally and figuratively, the notion that he would soon
reside in an exclusive area high above the city seemed to him
like a joke in search of a punch line. And that sense was
doubled, or perhaps tripled, when Petra Norris, who greeted
him upon his arrival with an iced tea and a smile, informed him
that she had already scheduled his first tennis lesson.
Though tempted to pinch himself, Calvin resisted for fear
that his ascent would somehow prove to be nothing more than a
dream.

If having a new, fashionable abode was a revelation to
Calvin, being at the wheel of something other than his clunker

was an even more dramatic change. Unsure whether to be self-conscious or proud, Calvin spent a half-hour enjoying the sights and curves of Mulholland Drive before finally yielding to responsibility and heading for Gadzooks.

There he parked the BMW with far more care than he ever gave to his VW, then headed down the stairs.

But as he stepped out of the garage, he spotted Amy Kawasaki, who looked anything but aglow.

"You're missing all the action," she said sarcastically.

"You?" Calvin asked, drawing an imaginary line across his throat.

"Not so far," said Amy with a sigh.

Opening the door to the Gadzooks offices, Calvin immediately heard the unmistakable and unhappy voice of Robert Williams, whose decibel level was off the charts.

"It's because I'm gay, goddamnit!" Robert screamed. "You're letting me go because I'm gay!"

Standing with Beverly Steele and Brad Tucker, Matt Donnelly shook his head.

"Not at all," Donnelly said softly.

Robert seethed. "Bullshit!" he hollered, pulling out his iPhone and starting to shoot video footage. "I'm getting all of you on camera for the lawsuit I'll be filing!"

"Film all you want," said Tucker. "But the cause will still be that you're a sniveling weasel who's done nothing positive."

Trying to be inconspicuous, Calvin attempted to slither past the crowd that had gathered, only to have Robert Williams point a finger at him.

"But this little shitbird from out of nowhere gets a fucking office?" Robert bellowed. "What do you have that I don't have?" he demanded of Calvin.

"Smarts," Calvin replied.

But that was not a sufficient answer for Robert, who glared first at Beverly Steele, then at Matt Donnelly, and finally at Brad Tucker.

"It's because he's straight, goddamnit! It's because the little prick is straight!"

Having escaped finally from Robert's histrionics, Calvin was heading down the hallway when Harley Brooks approached.

"Another one bites the dust," Harley said.

"Another one bites the dust," Calvin repeated.

"Not that I'll miss him. A creep born with a golden foot in his mouth and the personality of a toad."

Except for a trip to the park with Alonzo at lunchtime, Calvin kept a very low profile the rest of the day. Keeping his office door closed, he finished the work that Norris assigned, then spent some time reading profiles of the Gadzooks hierarchy, especially those he had gotten to know.

Still uncertain about where exactly he fit in, or what was expected of him at what he had started to think of as Casa Norris, Calvin hit a bar known for its free happy hour snacks once the work day was over. There he nursed a beer while attending to whatever food groups were satisfied by a constant flow of chicken wings, quesadillas, and pizza.

Only after the freebies were over, and rush hour traffic had subsided, did he finally head up to Mulholland Drive. There he made as inconspicuous an arrival as possible, avoiding the main house and slipping into his new lair.

Unaccustomed to the silence of the hills, Calvin turned on the flat screen TV in the guest house, which was a vast improvement over the ancient set at the motel. But despite the countless choices afforded by cable, there was nothing at all that captured his attention. Instead, he turned on his iPod and listened to the likes of Irma Thomas, Elmore James, and Ernie K-Doe. But even the music he loved failed to hold his interest.

Stretching out on the queen-sized bed, Calvin found himself ruminating on the strange trajectory that had led him, with stops in between, from his formative years in an area that subsequently became a full-fledged ghetto to a gilded spot overlooking all of Los Angeles.

His grammar school days were spent in a rapidly changing part of Newark, New Jersey, which for Calvin was the closest he had come to heaven. Thanks to population density, he had no play dates, car pools, or schedules. All he had to do was walk out the door in order to find scores of things to do, plus tons of kids with whom to do it all. Not surprisingly, it was not his father, nor was it coaches, who taught him how to play baseball, basketball, and football. His mentors were the older kids, who were always on the lookout for potential teammates.

That neighborhood was also where he began to acquire street smarts, thanks to an introduction into dice, poker, and, at the local candy store, the numbers racket.

More important, it was then and there that Calvin came to discover food that, in contrast his mother's offerings, actually had taste. First came a hotdog emporium called Syd's, which also served wonderfully appealing fat and greasy, heavily-salted fries. Then Vito's, where mouthwatering pizza sold by the slice led him to ridiculously yummy sausage-and-pepper subs. But best of all was a soul food restaurant run by a man named James together with his wife Mary. It was at their place that Calvin discovered revelations such as catfish, smothered chicken, and hush puppies, plus gumbo on Fridays and the world's best sweet potato pie. Making an even greater impression was the jukebox, which provided an introduction first to the likes of Wynonie Harris, Big Maybelle, Louis Jordan, and the Five Blind Boys of Mississippi, then later to lifelong favorites including Ray Charles, Dinah Washington, and the Harptones.

But what was a paradise for Calvin was anything but that for his parents, who dreamed incessantly about a home of their own. After the birth of a kid sister named Beth, then a year-and-a-half later a brother dubbed Brian, with the family's two-bedroom apartment no longer the slightest bit sufficient, the five of them moved to neighboring Elizabeth, where the spontaneity and freedom that had been so much a part of Calvin's life largely disappeared.

No longer could he have limitless options simply by

walking out the door. Nor were there countless other kids with whom to do this, that, or the other thing. Vanished, as well, was the food he had come to love, none of which was within walking distance of the new abode. Worst of all, the sole remaining source for the music he had come to cherish was black radio stations out of Newark and Harlem, since there was no soul food place nearby, and records were far too costly on his meager allowance.

Only when Calvin got to high school did he once again begin to find the kind of diversity he loved, plus, at last, greater access to his kind of food and music.

But by then, even that was no longer sufficient, which explained why what he came to call his *double life* led him more and more frequently into Greenwich Village, the East Village, and other parts of New York City.

Inevitably, it was that same longing, together with the same sense that there had to be more to life, that prompted Calvin to apply for the internship at Gadzooks.

That in turn, thanks to an unexpected series of events, was what ultimately led him to Mulholland Drive. There, after much rumination, plus some time spent listening to Lowell Fulson singing first "Reconsider Baby," then his version of "Tramp," Calvin fell asleep in a dwelling far, far away from Motel Hell.

The next day at work, instead of being happy and well rested, Calvin found himself feeling uncharacteristically jumpy. If having an office, a guest house, and a BMW were not sufficient to make him question who exactly he was, worse still was the awareness that he was about to add yet another dimension to his California metamorphosis.

The strange new realm that he was about to enter owed nothing to geography, but rather to self-image.

It was a tennis lesson that Calvin spent the better part of the day fretting about, for the simple reason that despite having acquired an education, plus an affinity for literature and film, he still viewed himself as a blue-collar guy, not someone who indulged in what, where he grew up, was dismissed as a country club sport.

Though he knew his jitters were silly, they nonetheless were troubling. Yet Calvin couldn't quite bring himself to discuss his feelings with either Alonzo or Carrie, let alone with Steve Norris or Petra.

So he stuck it out as best he could through the work day, then white-knuckled his way up the 405 to his new hilltop neighborhood.

Dressed in tennis whites that had miraculously appeared in the guest house, Calvin made progress on the court due to innate athleticism rather than anything resembling proper form or style as he gutted his way through his first lesson.

Despite himself, what he feared would be an ordeal proved at times to be fun, so that he was able to muster a smile when Petra Norris, with a margarita in hand, walked up through the backyard to observe.

Though he had agreed to have a drink with Petra afterward, those plans changed once the phone rang when he reentered the guest house for a shower.

To his surprise, it was Carrie on the other end.

"Busy?" she asked.

"Why?"

"Well, I was thinking –"

"Count me in!"

"But you didn't even hear –" she started to say, only to be interrupted by Calvin.

"Doesn't matter!"

An hour-and-a-half later, Calvin's BMW swung off the 10 Freeway at the Alameda exit, then wove its way through downtown streets until it pulled into a space on E. 6th Street. Walking around a homeless guy already sacked out on the ground, Calvin approached a bar called Varnish.

Willfully retro, with slatted-wood booths and a tile floor,

the place was populated mainly by hipsters when Calvin entered and looked around.

Spotting Carrie in a rear booth with a bottle of what proved to be a Chateau Montelena Cabernet in front of her, Calvin headed in that direction, then took a seat.

"Thanks for coming," Carrie said.

"Hey –"

"No, I mean it. You're a real friend."

"Exactly what I aspire to."

"Really?" Carrie asked, eyeing him strangely.

"What do you think?"

Carrie poured Calvin a glass of wine, which allowed them to toast. Only then did Carrie answer. "I think you're sweet to be keeping me company at a time when I need it."

"Things that bad?"

"Worse. That guy I told you I'd stopped seeing?"

"The one who got a second chance when genius here stood you up?"

Carrie shrugged. "Totally bonehead on my part. When I realized what a dumbbell I was, I ended it. Like we were ever going to move to New York!?"

"Ouch."

"What I want – what I'd love to try, at least – is to focus on designing. Not part-time, not off-hours, but 100%. He had this plan of getting a place in Lower Manhattan –"

"Really?"

"Or maybe even Brooklyn. Half-workshop for me, half-retail for my stuff. But I finally realized it was a sales pitch – words he knew I wanted to hear."

"So why so sad?"

"Because I let myself get taken in. Again. And –"

"Yeah?"

"A part of me misses him. That sound stupid?"

"It sounds like you're human."

"So what do I do?"

"Spend some time with someone who can help you get over it."

"Should I ask who?"

Calvin hoisted the bottle of wine and refilled their glasses.

"You could do worse," he said.

Carrie shrugged. "I don't think I'm ready for anything romantic."

"So what if it's purely physical?"

"Calvin!"

"Then let's just spend time together as friends."

"And see where it takes us?" Carrie asked, brightening.

Calvin nodded, then the two of them toasted once again.

"When?" Carrie asked.

"This weekend?"

"Deal."

"Great! So last question. If you could go anywhere in the world, where would it be?"

"Anywhere?"

"Anywhere."

"Xi'an," Carrie said.

"Where's that?"

"The place in China where my parents were born."

Calvin thought for a moment, then shrugged.

"Settle for someplace closer?"

The next morning, Jonathan Olson and Amy Kawasaki were walking nervously down the hall at Gadzooks when they saw Brad Tucker, who was clearly on a mission, storm by.

The two of them watched Tucker approach Calvin's new office, then drifted that way when he burst in.

Seated behind his desk, Calvin immediately looked up.

"Can I help you?" he asked.

"What do you think?"

"Well —"

Well, yes?" asked Tucker. "Or well, no?"

"It depends on what you need."

"*What*? How about *when*, for Chrissake?"

"When what?"

"When — this weekend."

"That's rough."

"Want to know rough? What's my name?"

"Brad Tucker."

"As in Tucker-the-stone-cold-motherfucker!"

"But, you see —"

Tucker stepped toward Calvin, then grabbed him by the shirt collar and nearly lifted him off the ground.

"No, dude – you see!"

Tucker pushed Calvin back into his chair.

"Now what exactly is your problem?" he then asked.

"I-it's just that I've got plans."

"Well, how about career plans? Just because you've got an office, that still doesn't mean dick. Read me?"

Calvin frowned.

"No way Donnelly, Kim, and that goddamn Norris get theirs, and yours truly doesn't!" Tucker snarled. "Hear me? No fucking way!"

Catching her breath post-breakfast rush, Carrie was sipping a cup of tea when Calvin walked into the restaurant.

"You a beach guy?" Carrie asked.

"Why?"

"I was thinking that maybe Saturday —"

Seeing Calvin frown, Carrie darkened.

"What?" she asked.

"It's just that —"

"It's off?"

"Not off, exactly —"

"On hold?"

"I can explain."

"No explanation necessary."

"It's kind of like —"

Carrie held up a hand to stop him.

"I'm getting used to it," she said.

That evening, carrying a bottle of Dom Perignon and two champagne flutes, Petra Norris, in a slinky dress, stepped out of her back door, then headed across the yard toward the guest house.

Feeling glum, Calvin was trying to lose himself in a televised ball game when he heard a knock on the door.

"It's open," he yelled.

As Calvin got up, in stepped Petra.

"Time to celebrate our new arrangement," she said.

"B-but –"

"What if Mr. Cool comes home? Relax. Thursday night's when he and his buddies head over to Koreatown for kimchi and coochie-coo. Which means –"

To illustrate her point, Petra opened the Dom Perignon like a pro, then filled the two flutes.

"Look, I'm not sure –" Calvin mumbled.

Ignoring his resistance, Petra handed him some bubbly.

"Please don't play naïve," she said. "My husband put you here to babysit for me. So even if nothing happens, he'll assume it did."

"B-but –"

"But, nothing. What it means is that we might as well enjoy ourselves. Right?"

Without giving Calvin a chance to answer, Petra moved in and kissed him, then looked him in the eye.

"Besides," she said, "isn't business supposed to have its perks?"

Putting down her Champagne flute, Petra began to undress him.

The next day at noon, Alonzo Steven, basketball in hand, stepped out of the Gadzooks building and found Calvin seated on a bench.

"Ruderman," Alonzo said, "what up?"

Calvin's only response was a sigh.

"Looks to me," Alonzo continued, "like you've got a heavy-duty case of *Be careful what you wish for.* How about some b-ball to cure what ails you?"

"Guess who's about to go on-duty. And anyway, I'd need

something a whole lot stronger than that. Know what I was thinking?"

"I give up."

"Of the many routes to success?"

"Yeah?"

"Seems like I chose the vaginal."

Less than an hour later, a familiar-looking Lincoln Town Car was headed east on Santa Monica Boulevard when Jose the driver leaned back toward Calvin.

"Mind if I say something?" Jose asked.

"Fire away."

"I've been driving like this for some time now, chauffeuring movie stars, rock stars, the whole nine, so I thought I'd seen everything. But you? I don't know how in hell you do it, but when it comes to pretty ladies – man, you're the king! So who's on for this weekend – or do you want to surprise me?"

"What's life without surprises?" Calvin replied.

Ten minutes later, the Lincoln turned onto a quiet street in West Hollywood, then pulled up in front of a nondescript low-rise apartment.

By no means a novice any longer, Calvin entered the building with a well-earned *Been there, done that* attitude, then climbed the stairs to the second floor. Reaching his destination, he rang the bell.

Seconds passed, then to Calvin's surprise the door was opened by a thin, effervescent young guy whose photo could appear beside the word *Twinkee* in a slang dictionary.

"I'm looking for Sandy," a startled Calvin muttered.

"And you got him! Puerto Rico, here we come!"

As always, Jose the driver was standing beside the open trunk of the Town Car when Calvin reappeared. But where previously he had done his best to play it cool, giving Calvin a surreptitious wink or some other sign of approval, this time

Jose found himself struggling to keep from gaping.

Calvin, meanwhile, looked like he was dying a thousand deaths. But not Sandy, who was bubbling with enthusiasm.

"*Perfecto!*" he gushed at the sight of the Town Car. "I love traveling in style!"

Despite Sandy's attempts to engage him in conversation, Calvin was beyond monosyllabic on the trip to the airport, then even more laconic as the two of them waited in the VIP lounge.

Not the least bit daunted, Sandy was still of good cheer when both of them finally boarded the jet, then took their seats in Business Class.

"So my understanding is that nights in San Juan," he stated, "the two of us will be joined at the hip."

When Calvin's only reply was a frown, Sandy took no umbrage.

"Gotta warn you about something," Sandy said.

"What's that?"

"I am what's known as irrepressible."

Despite himself, Calvin laughed. "Sure fooled me."

It was evening by the time another Lincoln Town Car made its way through traffic in Puerto Rico so as to pull up at the scenic El San Juan Hotel & Spa.

Once more Sandy gushed.

"*Perfecto!*" he again exclaimed.

Fighting a kind of self-consciousness that owed to his years in blue collar New Jersey, Calvin walked through the crowded lobby and up to the check-in desk with Sandy by his side.

"Calvin Sands from Gadzooks," he quietly informed the desk clerk.

"*Perfecto*, Senor Sands," replied the desk clerk, checking out the two of them. "We have a lovely ocean view for the two of you with a king-sized bed. *Muy bonito.*"

While Calvin cringed, Sandy beamed.

Just a couple of minutes later, the door to an ocean-view room was unlocked, then in stepped a baggage-wielding bellhop, followed by Calvin and Sandy.

The two of them watched as the bellhop turned on the lights, then carefully deposited their suitcases.

"*Es todo?*" asked the bellhop. "Anything else?"

Shaking his head, Calvin handed the bellhop a tip.

"*Buenas noches,*" came the response. "Pleasant dreams."

As the bellhop left, closing the door behind him, Sandy smiled at Calvin.

"And then there were two," he said.

Calvin could not keep himself from squirming. "Let's get something straight –"

"Honey, there's not a whole lot straight about me –"

"But –"

"No worries, okay?"

"If you don't mind my asking, how come?"

"I promised dickhead I'd be monogamous."

"Dickhead?"

Sandy nodded.

"As in personality, not anatomy," he explained. "I mean, did he tip you that *Sandy* wasn't someone who sits down to pee?"

Calvin shook his head.

"See?" Sandy continued. "So relax. And if I do anything to you while you're sleeping, I promise it won't be too much."

"W-what?"

"Just joking. But when we get back to LA –"

"Yeah?"

"I've got great Bette Midler tickets if you want to join me."

Sandy laughed. So, too, did Calvin.

Though the weekend proved to be far less excruciating than he feared, with Sandy a surprisingly good dinner companion who, it turned out, shared his views about politics,

Billie Holiday, and even Ethiopian food, Calvin was nonetheless far from happy.

By day, his thoughts were largely about Carrie, who failed to return his multiple calls and texts.

By night, what went through his mind was far darker, but not because Sandy was curled up in bed beside him.

Initially Calvin tried to use his customary list-making as a coping mechanism. First came an attempt to rank the ten most embarrassing experiences of his life. When that was of no help, the next try was to compile his ten worst all-time dates. But ultimately, in the wee small hours of both Friday and Saturday, what haunted Calvin more than anything else was the realization that he was in effect two different people.

Though occasional moments of doubt were inevitable, in waking hours he was for the most part the person he wanted to be: brash, caustic, iconoclastic. Thanks to the street smarts he had acquired over the years, he was largely able to be funny, irreverent, and more or less the Calvin of his choosing.

But at 3 AM or so, he started to understand, the defense mechanisms that otherwise enabled him to cope were largely non-existent.

Such thinking reminded him of something said not by Bo Diddley or Irma Thomas or any other singer whose words he took to heart, but instead by a French existentialist whose work he read in college. When asked if he was comfortable denying the existence of God, Albert Camus was quoted as saying, "Yes, except sometimes in the middle of the night."

Week Six

MONDAY MORNING, Calvin arrived at Gadzooks earlier than ever before, so as to sneak into his office without being waylaid at Cash & Carrie by Brad Tucker.

Seated behind his desk, he was trying to focus on demographics when, after a knock, in stepped Harlan Brooks III, dressed as though ready to audition for a remake of "The Wild One."

"Busy?" Harley asked.

"Hard at work solving all the world's problems. What's up?"

"Just wanted to say goodbye."

"You got bounced?" Calvin asked with genuine shock.

"Beating 'em to the punch. Even if they don't realize it's the wrong fit, I do."

Distressed, Calvin stood. "I'm really sorry."

"Don't be," said Harley with a shrug. "When you come down to it, sitting behind a desk is not what I'm meant to do. And besides, there's a part of me that always wanted to ride off into the sunset. But there's something important I've got to say."

"Okay."

"I'm proud of you."

"How come?"

"The odds were stacked against you from Day One, but you never let the shits get you down."

As the two of them hugged, into the office stepped Jonathan Olson.

"Speaking of shits," said Harley.

Ignoring the put-down, Jonathan coldly addressed Calvin.

"It seems that Wesley Phillips for some reason wants you," he stated with a not fully masked sneer.

"And a certain preppy asshole is jealous as can be," Harley commented.

"Fuck you, loser!" snarled Jonathan.

"Want to step outside?" Harley demanded.

"You're hardly worth it," Mr. Oil Spill spat.

Watching him turn his back disdainfully and leave, Harley and Calvin shared one last laugh.

Walking down the hall several minutes later, Imran Habib and Samantha Steinberg tried unsuccessfully to make eye contact with Calvin, whose mind was elsewhere as he neared Wesley Phillips' suite.

Opening the door, Calvin approached one of the CEO's two assistants.

"I'm Calvin Sands," he said.

"Go right in," said the older of the two women, whose name plate said: *Stella.*

With a knock, Calvin stepped into Wesley Phillips' inner office, which clearly was the domain of someone who denied himself nothing. There was sports memorabilia galore, including autographed baseballs, basketballs, and footballs, plus photos of Phillips with the likes of Michael Jordan, Peyton Manning, and Clayton Kershaw. From the world of music, there was a signed Jimi Hendrix guitar, as well as a blown-up and personalized photo of Solomon Burke on-stage with Mick Jagger. Plus there were all sorts of framed portaits and laminated plaques related to Gadzooks highlights.

With a bunch of documents in hand, Wesley Phillips waved Calvin in.

"I gather you're a guy with quite a future," Phillips stated.

"Well —"

"No false modesty, please. I've got strong recommendations here from George Kim, Matt Donnelly, Brad Tucker, and the king of cool, Steve Norris."

Phillips flipped theatrically through the paperwork.

"According to them," he said, "you're bright... diligent... resourceful... and a team player... Make you feel good?"

"I suppose."

"But there's one trait they forgot. You're also extremely

popular."

Wesley Phillips studied Calvin, who made no effort to respond. Suddenly there was a knock, then the office door swung open.

"Got a quick sec?" asked Beverly Steele.

Wesley Phillips waved his hand dismissively. "Not now."

Beverly left instantly, shutting the door behind her.

"When   four   key   execs   write   unsolicited recommendations," Phillips then said to Calvin, "isn't that proof you're popular?"

"I-I guess."

"And ordinarily I'd like that. Except –"

Calvin grew even more apprehensive as Phillips allowed for a moment of silence.

"Ever heard of Jim LeGrand?" Phillips finally continued.

Calvin shook his head no.

"He's a guy who was popular here," Phillips went on. "Why? Because he was taking book. Horse races, football, elections, you name it. And before him there was a guy named Charles Goldsmith. Turns out he was running a full-scale pharmacy: Ecstacy, poppers, pills, whatever. So what's your angle?"

"Nothing."

"Right, and I never heard of Ruderman, either. Just so you know, I fired a certain benefactor of yours. Want to guess who?"

"I suspect you'll tell me."

"The one and only Steve Norris. Why do you think that was?"

Once more Calvin shook his head.

"To avoid a potential lawsuit from the intern he was banging," Phillips explained. "Who, by the way, has also been let go."

Wesley Phillips paused and smiled.

"Get the feeling I have some sense of what's going on around here?" he asked a moment later.

Calvin responded affirmatively.

"Just to set the record straight," Phillips then said, "I've been looking for an excuse to can Norris for some time now. First, for paying more attention to his dick than to his work. And second, because there's nothing like a good firing to keep everybody else on their toes. Make sense?"

Calvin nodded with little zeal.

"And here's another kernel of wisdom for you," Phillips added. "Want to hear the truth about someone – like Norris – who tries so hard to be hip?"

"Okay."

"He isn't. But since this means that you're effectively homeless," Phillips stated, "the good news is he's not the only one with a guest house. And the one I have is yours – plus a salary – if you play ball the right way. Clear?"

"Yes."

"Good. Give some thought to what I said, then we'll take it from there."

His head spinning, Calvin started toward the door, only to be stopped a moment later.

"Oh, one thing, Calvin –"

Calvin turned so as to face Phillips. "Yes?"

"What are you doing this weekend?"

Calvin's jaw dropped. But to his dismay, Wesley Phillips immediately burst into laughter.

"Only joking," Phillips said. "Only joking."

Moments later, Alonzo Stevens was walking down the hallway when he spotted Calvin approaching.

"Somebody looks mighty discombobulated," Alonzo said.

"No shit."

"Seems to me like b-ball at lunch is the perfect remedy."

Instead of responding in a positive way, Calvin merely shrugged.

Still dazed, Calvin was daydreaming as noon approached when into his office, without either a warning or a knock, stepped George Kim, followed by Matt Donnelly and Brad

Tucker.

"Three cool cats," Calvin said at the sight of them with precious little warmth.

"Three horny cats who've never received one word of thanks," responded George Kim.

"That what you want?" Calvin asked.

"With Norris gone," interjected Donnelly, "we want to make sure your lips are sealed."

"Done."

"And," added Donnelly, "we want some more *bearding*."

"Not happening."

"Remember, dude," said Tucker, "we made you, and we can break you."

"Think so?"

"We know so," Donnelly affirmed. "And the three of us are about to –"

Before Donnelly could finish his sentence, another voice was suddenly heard.

"About to what?" asked Wesley Phillips, entering Calvin's office.

"C-congratulate Calvin on his promotion," George Kim stammered.

"A well deserved promotion, if I dare say so," stated Wesley Phillips. "Now if you'll excuse us –"

To the amazement of the three lesser-ranking execs, the CEO ushered Calvin toward the door.

Headed toward Calvin's office with a basketball in hand, Alonzo Stevens was surprised to see his friend emerging together with Wesley Phillips.

With Alonzo watching, off the CEO and Calvin started in the other direction, until, that is, Beverly Steele's assistant Arthur approached.

"Excuse me, Mr. P –" Arthur said deferentially.

"Not now."

A few minutes later, Calvin was riding shotgun in a 1964 ½

Mustang convertible with Wesley Phillips at the wheel.

"Know who you remind me of?" the CEO asked as they headed east.

"I hope not those guys you mentioned."

"Me when I was getting started. That's not so bad, is it?"

"Not so bad? It's really flattering."

Up toward Sunset they drove, then east toward Brentwood, where they turned onto Mandeville Canyon Road.

In this surprisingly rustic setting, Wesley Phillips swung the car onto a long, winding driveway, then up they came to what could only be described as an estate.

If the Norris place was impressive to Calvin, the Phillips property was absolutely overwhelming: a wonderland with a stream, horses, a tennis court, and an Olympic-sized pool.

Calvin could not help but gape as Wesley Phillips parked near an incredible collection of vintage automobiles, then led him past a house that resembled the chateau at Fountainebleau until they reached a guest house that made his previous abode look like a shanty.

"Think you can make do here?" Wesley Phillips asked with a wink.

"Mr. Phillips –"

"Wes –" Phillips corrected.

Tongue-tied, Calvin said nothing further.

"I suppose you want to know why," Phillips continued.

"If you're willing to say."

"People assume I'm creative," Phillips remarked. "But the truth is, I haven't got a single creative bone in my whole goddamn body."

"But –"

"What it doesn't say in my bio is that I've got an antenna. When something – or someone – has got it, I get a funny kind of buzz. I personally couldn't create a computer, or even a dog house. Fact is, I'm both literally and figuratively all thumbs. And it's especially true with technologies... apps... whatever. But Gadzooks came about because before anyone knew the difference between a search engine and a fried egg, yours truly recognized an opportunity. And that's how I am when it comes to manpower as well. Read me?"

"I guess."

"I need somebody who's smarter than all those self-styled geniuses around me. Somebody who's going places. And gets it. Someone I can trust. You up for that?"

"I can try."

Wesley Phillips extended a hand, and the two of them shook.

"But as for this weekend," said Phillips, "I wasn't completely joking. Got a passport?"

Calvin nodded. "I once did volunteer work in Costa Rica."

"Nice. You're going to a conference in Puerto Vallarta – but not as my beard. In fact, I think you should bring a date. On me. Sound good?"

Calvin nodded again.

"See," explained Phillips, "my wife's headed to Sacramento for some political thing. And since I don't feel like traveling solo, having you cover for me means I can make like I'm young and irresponsible."

"Anything special I need to do?"

"Other than don't drink the water? Yeah, get some for me."

Wesley Phillips chuckled, then spotted a very attractive woman in her forties approaching.

"Here comes my beautiful wife now. Calvin Sands, my wonderful wife Jenny. Honey, say hello to the bright young guy I was telling you about."

"Pleased to meet you," Calvin said.

"Pleasure's mine," Jenny Phillips replied. "You'll like the guest house. So tell me, you guys hungry?"

Seeing Calvin's reluctance to answer, it was Wesley Phillips who spoke.

"Aside from being an avid conservationist and force in the community – as well as a great wife and mother – Jenny, here, happens to be one of the world's great cooks."

"Somebody," said Jenny, "is known to exaggerate."

"Know what they say in England?" Phillips asked Calvin rhetorically. "No man is a hero to his wife or his valet."

That afternoon, with the lunch crowd having departed, Carrie was straightening up Cash & Carrie when Calvin popped in.

"Still mad at me?" he asked.

"How can I be mad at a guy who's been taken under the CEO's wing?"

"Are you in the CIA or something?"

"Why?"

"Sometimes I feel like you not only know a whole lot more than I do, but you've gotten to know it weeks in advance. Okay, serious question for you. Got a passport?"

"Why?"

"Since there are certain things called perks —"

"Yeah?"

"How about joining me for a weekend in Puerto Vallarta?"

"I thought we were taking it slow."

"Sure, slow margaritas. Slow swims in warm water. Slow meals and hikes —"

"Nothing else?"

Calvin shrugged. "A guy can hope. But even if it's just for companionship —"

Carrie leaned toward Calvin and kissed him on the cheek.

"You're on."

Jonathan Olson was approaching Cash & Carrie when Calvin stepped outside a couple of moments later.

"Bet you're trying to get some slant-eyed twat," Jonathan joked in a lame attempt to curry favor.

Calvin tensed. "Tell me I didn't hear that."

Instead of correctly reading Calvin's ire, Mr. Oil Spill didn't retreat at all.

"Lighten up, bro," he said. "We'd all like some of that sweet Chinese pussy."

For Calvin, time suddenly seemed to stop as he eyed

Jonathan, who was far more imposing physically, standing 6'3"
with muscles developed during his years playing lacrosse.

Then suddenly, despite clearly being over-matched, Calvin
let loose with a roundhouse right that knocked his smug
nemesis off his feet!

The rest of the week proved to be surprisingly pleasant for
Calvin. Part of that owed to Gadzooks being a hotbed of
gossip, which meant that in record time Calvin was given the
kind of respect once reserved for championship boxers like
Manny Pacquiao, Oscar De La Hoya, or even Muhammed Ali.

But even more important was the simple fact that for the
first time since Calvin's arrival in Southern California, the
weekend ahead was filled with anticipation rather than dread,
and with excitement instead of chagrin.

As a result, half of his free time was spent preparing
himself physically by running, doing pushes and crunches, and
even climbing up and down the celebrated Santa Monica steps,
all in the hope that he might manage to look good in a bathing
suit. What time was left was dedicated to another kind of
preparation: things he could do with – and say to – Carrie
during their time together in Mexico.

And all the while he was adjusting not simply to life at
Chateau Phillips, but also to the fact that Wesley seemed
determined to groom him as both a protege and a pal.

Friday morning found Calvin, not for the first time, seated
in a familiar Lincoln Town Car as it fought its way east on
Sunset Boulevard until it finally reached Silverlake.

There it turned onto a street near the reservoir, then
turned again and pulled up in front of a funky old three-story
apartment building.

Without a word this time, Jose the driver watched as
Calvin, with never before seen effervescence, jumped out of
the car, then strolled merrily toward the front door.

Then upstairs he bounded, straight to the third floor until
he reached his destination, where he knocked expectantly.

When nothing happened, an undeterred Calvin knocked again, then rang the bell.

When still nothing happened, Calvin pulled out his iPhone and dialed a number, then frowned when he got voicemail.

"This is Calvin, wondering where you are," he stated emphatically. "Call me, please."

As always, Jose the driver was standing beside the open trunk of the Town Car when Calvin, clearly alarmed, stepped out of the building alone.

"Problems?" Jose asked.

"Let's go to the office," Calvin replied.

Both men climbed back into the Lincoln for a trip that seemed to take far longer than it actually did, and was spent in silence except for Calvin periodically hitting *redial* on his phone.

By the time the Town Car reached the Gadzooks building, Calvin was in full-scale panic mode. Bolting from the vehicle, he sprinted into Cash & Carrie, then approached the counter, where he found May standing alone.

"Carrie here?" Calvin instantly asked.

"No," May replied.

"Any idea what happened to her?"

"She called last night to say she was driving up the coast."

Crestfallen, Calvin trudged wearily toward the Lincoln, where Jose was waiting behind the wheel.

"To the airport?" Jose asked once Calvin had climbed into the back seat.

"Either there or a gun shop."

Like a sleepwalker, Calvin went through security at LAX, then sat almost catatonic in the VIP lounge. But by the time he boarded a Delta jet, then sat in Business Class beside an empty seat, he was fuming.

Nor did the steaming subside despite the number of

cocktails he consumed on his flight south of the border.

When he got to Puerto Vallarta, however, his ire had given way to a combination of uselessness, hopelessness, and depression.

Though aware that being melodramatic would lead nowhere good, Calvin could not stop himself from debating what was worse, being jilted, or having to spend what had promised to be a wonderful weekend gloomily, frustratingly alone.

Nor was his mood lightened when, after a lonely, solitary dinner at the beautiful Hacienda San Angel where he was staying, he took a stroll under the moonlight on the indescribably romantic beach behind his hotel.

Unwilling to yield to emptiness, Calvin put on his shoes and wandered toward the Hacienda's front entrance, where he had a doorman hail him a cab.

"*Si, senor?*" the cabbie asked as Calvin climbed into the back seat.

"Margaritas," Calvin announced. "*Mucho* margaritas."

An hour later, at a cantina in downtown Puerto Vallerta, as a strolling mariachi band passed by, Calvin downed what was decidedly not his first margarita of the evening, then spotted a *senorita* of a certain age a couple of bar stools away.

Trying to be suave, Calvin leaned toward her, nearly falling off his stool in the process.

"Join me?" Calvin asked.

The senorita smiled, so Calvin turned toward the bartender.

"*Dos mas, por favor.*"

After too many more rounds of margaritas, Calvin and the senorita staggered out of the cantina.

"Now I buy you the best tacos in Mexico," the senorita, whose name Calvin had still not learned, announced.

"The best?"

"*Los mejores des todos!*"

Off they wandered away from the touristy part of town toward an alley where the two of them came upon a stand clearly not featured in "Lonely Planet" or on internet sites discussing where to eat while south of the border.

His inhibitions having been washed away along with his sense of hygiene, Calvin allowed himself to be coaxed into eating tacos filled with mystery meat and other untranslatables, which to his surprise proved to be not just greasy but tasty as well.

"*Listo*?" asked the senorita seductively, placing her hand on Calvin's thigh.

"Ready as can be!"

Up toward the Hacienda San Angel came a taxi, then out stepped Calvin together with the senorita. With romance, or at least lust, seemingly imminent, Calvin handed the cabdriver some pesos, then suddenly let out a scream!

To the dismay of the senorita, but not the doormen, all of whom had seen such behavior among *gringos* before, Calvin made a mad dash into the hotel!

Early the following morning, a doctor carrying a leather bag knocked on Calvin's villa door.

"I am *el medico*," he said. "The doctor."

Looking green at the gills, Calvin flushed the toilet, as he had done far too many times during the night, then pulled up his pants and stumbled to the door.

The moment Calvin opened it, the doctor sized up the situation.

"You have heard of Montezuma?" he asked.

"Yeah."

"We call this his revenge."

With that pronouncement, any chance Calvin had for a good time in Mexico promptly vanished.

It was near midnight on Sunday when, after bathroom stops at an In-And-Out Burger, a McDonald's, and a

Walgreen's, up toward Chateau Phillips came the Lincoln Town Car, which dropped Calvin off in front.

Still more than a trifle seasick, Calvin was in the process of trudging toward the guest house when he heard a voice.

"The world traveler!" announced Wesley Phillips.

Calvin turned to see the CEO, who had obviously been drinking, approaching with a wine glass in hand.

"I envy you," Phillips said.

"How come?"

"The world is yours. No responsibilities, no obligations. Girls. Good times. All the stuff that I missed."

Calvin put down his suitcase and studied Phillips.

"Missed how?"

"By being so goddamn serious from the day I was born. I was so busy trying to get there – wherever the hell *there* was – that it left no time for fun. And look what it got me."

"Everything everybody dreams of."

"Hype, Calvin. Media bullshit and hype. *Wesley Phillips, the man who's got it all.* Great wife, great kids, great art collection, great antique cars, great Laker, Clipper, and Dodger seats. But where's the excitement? The friends? The laughs? It's life in a gilded cage."

"Then why not change?"

"I've been dreaming about it for years. First, it was when the kids are old enough. Then, when they're out of high school. But now, even with both of them in college, it's always *I don't want to hurt Jenny*, or *I have to pick the right moment*, or some other stall tactic. And you know what makes it worse?"

Calvin shook his head.

"I'm in love," Phillips admitted.

"What's wrong with that?"

"With somebody else."

Calvin forced himself to keep from reacting.

"Don't get me wrong," Phillips went on. "I love Jenny. Always have, and always will. But with this other girl, I'm in love *and* in lust. I walk around hearing whistles and bells. Corny, huh?"

When Calvin failed to respond, Phillips studied him for a moment.

"You're wondering why I'm laying this on you," the CEO then said.

"To some degree."

"To some degree, my ass! So tell me, what's your fall-back?"

"My what?"

"Every intern who starts with us has some kind of fall-back in case they get cut. Tell me yours?"

"I don't know."

"There's got to be something."

"I guess teaching in the inner city."

"Commendable."

"Says he with undisguised scorn."

"Anything but. Generally, it's *To go into Daddy's business*, or *To write the great American screenplay*."

"Which, I guess, makes me weird."

"In a good way. But it makes this an even more important moment. This is your chance to decide who you are, and who you want to be. If you want to be the do-gooder instead of winding up like me, here's your opportunity to run for it by getting out now."

"And if I don't?"

"Then you know what? It'll be your chance for the brass ring *and* the pussy that goes with it."

Week Seven

EARLY THE NEXT MORNING, Jenny Phillips was in the backyard trimming rose bushes when Calvin semi-staggered from the guest house.

"Feeling better?" she asked.

Still not feeling fully awake or alive, Calvin mustered a half-nod.

"Sorry, my husband tried to bend your ear last night," Jenny continued. "For a guy who never said much, he's turning into a chatterbox. Guess it's his way of adjusting to the empty nest. That's why it's good you're here. Gives him someone to talk to."

"You two don't talk much?"

"About what? With both kids off to college, it's either his work, which never exactly gave me goose bumps, or my charity efforts, which he, for want of a better term, accepts."

Jenny shrugged.

"At least we're still friends," she added. "Which is more than most couples. How about you? Got a girlfriend?"

"I wish."

"No need to rush. Sometimes I wonder what would've happened if we didn't have kids so soon."

Calvin watched Jenny ponder that thought for a moment.

"Offer you some coffee?" she then asked.

"Some other time?"

"Okay."

Calvin consciously avoided Cash & Carrie when he arrived at the Gadzooks building, making his way directly into his office. Still very much under the weather, he sat there in silence with the door closed until, at 10:15, there was a knock.

"Come in," Calvin said.

In popped Samantha Steinberg.

"So do I now call you Mr. Sands?" she asked.

"Either that or Your Majesty. What's up?"

"Your presence is requested in Head-Honcho-Ville."

Ten minutes later, Rolando Dango was in the hallway when he saw Jonathan Olson approaching with a swagger.

"Somebody's looking pretty cocky," Rolando stated.

"When the big boss calls, it's got to be good. Right?"

Not even waiting for an answer, Mr. Oil Spill strode toward Wesley Phillips' suite.

Stepping in, he approached the two assistants.

"Jonathan Olson, here as requested," he announced proudly.

"Go right in," replied Stella, the senior assistant.

Entering Wesley Phillips private domain, Jonathan Olson's air of confidence took an instant hike when he realized that the CEO, instead of being alone, was accompanied by Calvin Sands of all people.

Nonetheless, it was Wesley Phillips – and Wesley Phillips alone – whom Jonathan addressed.

"You wish to see me?" he asked.

To Jonathan's dismay, it was the person he was trying to ignore – Calvin – who responded.

"Despite what you think," Calvin said, "arrogance is far from appealing."

"Why is he speaking?" Mr. Oil Spill promptly demanded of Wesley Phillips.

"Because I asked him to," the CEO replied.

"So your *Who's-Who* dad got you into Princeton," Calvin stated, "and that makes you feel special. But know what I think?"

"I can't wait to hear –"

"Just because you were born in the end zone, that doesn't mean you scored a touchdown. Your snooty bullshit is reason enough to boot your ass out. But worse, you've done nothing positive or constructive – I mean zero! – to distinguish yourself in any meaningful way."

Jonathan turned to Wesley Phillips. "Is this your verdict?

Or his?"

"Both," the CEO said with an icy smile.

Suddenly no longer a study in haughtiness, Jonathan Olson turned beseechingly to Calvin.

"Can't we talk about this?" he begged.

"Know what? I'm not available for that."

A couple of moments later, Rolando Dango who was dawdling in the hallway, spotted Jonathan Olson leaving Wesley Phillips' suite.

"So?" he asked.

Unwilling to cop to the truth, Jonathan faked a smile.

"I told 'em to go fuck themselves," he said with false pride.

Wesley Phillips, meanwhile, threw some papers into his attache case, then turned to Calvin.

"Somebody like his first taste of power?" the CEO said.

Calvin merely shrugged.

"Might as well admit it," Phillips urged.

"Okay, you got me."

"Just be careful –"

"How so?"

"It becomes an addiction."

"C'mon –"

"Trust me. More than chocolate, maybe even more than heroin or sex, once you've tasted blood – I mean really tasted blood the way you just did – it's hard not to want more. Can you tell me truthfully – I mean from your heart of hearts – that it wasn't a rush unlike any other?"

Calvin pondered for a moment, then shrugged again.

"Given a chance," Phillips continued, "everybody – and I mean everybody – cherishes the opportunity to become a vampire. Think about that for a moment or two, then there's something else I want you to do. Ready?"

"Ready."

"Gather yourself, then go down to your office and get your stuff."

"Can I ask why?" Calvin inquired with more than a bit of concern.

"Because it's playtime."

Not long thereafter, Alonzo Stevens was headed toward Calvin's office when Calvin approached from the other direction.

"Got a sec?" Alonzo asked.

To Alonzo's dismay, Calvin waved him off in a fashion far too reminiscent of Wesley Phillips.

"Not now."

Noon found Calvin somewhere he'd never been before, on a fishing boat out in the ocean north of Malibu.

With the wind blowing through their hair, he and Wesley Phillips, with fishing rods in action, seemed almost like salts of the sea.

"Do this often?" Calvin asked, breaking an extended silence.

"Hardly ever."

"Too busy?"

Wesley Phillips shook his head. "No fun doing it alone."

"Why's it have to be alone?"

"Because," the CEO said with more than a trace of sadness, "nearly everybody in the world wants a piece of me."

Just shy of 4 PM, a '57 Chevy convertible zoomed south on Pacific Coast Highway with fishing rods in the rear, then swung up toward a funky seafood shack.

Out stepped Wesley Phillips and Calvin, who entered the joint and ordered, then were delighted when, just a few minutes later, a pretty waitress brought them a platter of crab.

The CEO took pleasure in watching the young waitress's behind as she wandered off, then turned to Calvin.

"So this *bearding* you were doing," he began, "how exactly did it work?

"In Miami, or Seattle, or wherever, I'd pinch hit at the conference by day –"

"Then babysit the date at night?"

"Exactly."

"And what about getting to the airport?" Phillips asked.

"A Town Car would pick me up, then we'd go and get the great-and-good friend."

"This time, let's change things."

"Huh?" asked Calvin.

"You'll get picked up at the office."

"W-what do you mean?"

"Just my luck Jenny loves Chinese food and wants to see the Great Wall."

"I think I'm missing something."

"We're going to Beijing, Calvin. And wouldn't you know it, the whole gang's on the same damn flight. Jenny and I are in First – you and my little sweetie are in Business – and, because there were no other seats, poor Beverly's squeezed into Coach."

"Beverly?"

"Taking care of a little this, that, and the other thing," Phillips stated. Then, with a wink, he added, "Plus, the more the merrier. Right?"

Calvin's only response was a gulp.

Early Friday morning, Jose the driver was standing beside the Lincoln Town Car when Calvin emerged from the Gadzooks building, suitcase in hand.

"Guess someone got his groove back," Jose said softly as Calvin approached.

Not certain what that was supposed to mean, Calvin handed Jose his suitcase, then opened the back door and got the shock of his life.

Seated in the rear was none other than Carrie!

For a moment, time stood still. Then two people gasped simultaneously.

"You?!" said both Carrie and Calvin.

Oblivious to what was going on, Jose the driver climbed behind the wheel.

"You lovebirds ready?" he asked.

Before either of them could respond, Jose hit the gas and pulled out into traffic.

As the Town Car fought its way through rush hour messiness, in the back seat silence reigned – strained, uncomfortable, frigid silence between Carrie and Calvin that made each block seem like a mile, and each mile seem like it was taking forever.

At long last, up toward the International Terminal came the Lincoln, which deftly cut through the mass of cars, limos, buses, and vans, then pulled up at the curb.

Still giving each other the icicle treatment, Carrie and Calvin climbed out of the back seat, then took the baggage handed to them by Jose, who still had no clue as to what was transpiring, or why.

"Don't do anything I wouldn't do," he said.

Neither Calvin nor Carrie deigned to reply.

Amongst people heading to the farthest corners of the globe, Calvin and Carrie entered the Tom Bradley Terminal.

Suddenly, spontaneously, the two of them stopped and faced each other.

"I can't believe –" Calvin started to say, only to be interrupted by Carrie.

"Don't get high and mighty with me!"

"What in hell does that mean?"

"Think I don't know the secret to your rapid rise?"

"Least I haven't been banging somebody old and married!"

"Oh yeah? What would Mrs. Norris say?"

Calvin cringed, then banged his fist against a wall.

"That's it!" he yelled. "You're on your own!"

"Bullshit," said Carrie.

"Says who?"

"You're too goddamn ambitious to walk."

Calvin took a deep breath. "You'd like that, wouldn't you?

To see me give up everything I've gotten."

"All the stuff that's making the world a much better place."

"Well –"

"Well, what?"

"At least now we know."

"Know what?"

"Who won the pool to get into your pants."

Before Carrie, who was clearly shaken, could muster a reply, another voice was heard.

"Excited about the trip?" asked Wesley Phillips.

Both Carrie and Calvin turned to see the CEO approaching together with his wife Jenny.

"Jenny, you know Calvin of course," said Phillips, seemingly the epitome of grace. "And Jenny, Carrie – Carrie, Jenny."

Both Calvin and Carrie were stunned by Wesley Phillips' ability to handle the introductions as though they were not merely normal, but totally natural. Yet that didn't stop the two women from eyeing each other strangely, though neither one uttered even a word.

Then up stepped someone who instantly broke the tension: Beverly Steele.

"Can somebody point me toward China?" she joked.

Despite everything that was going on – or perhaps because of it – the five of them shared a much-needed laugh.

Not quite two hours later, as the China Air jet was still in its early stages of the lengthy flight, Jenny Phillips turned to her husband, who was seated comfortably beside her in the First Class cabin.

"I thought you said Calvin didn't have a girlfriend," she said.

"You know how it is with kids," Phillips improvised, doing his best to mask his discomfort. "First it's *Hey?* or *What up?*, then two minutes later it's *Wanna hook up?*"

"But how'd you know her name?"

"Carrie? From Cash & Carrie in our building? Of course

I know her name. Are you upset about something?"

"Me? Why should I be upset when they're so obviously in love?"

The CEO studied his wife, unable to determine if – or to what degree – Jenny was being sarcastic, suspicious, or both.

Meanwhile, in Business Class, Calvin and Carrie were busy doing silent burns.

And in Coach, Beverly squirmed unhappily between a Chinese woman who was snoring and a fat American who alternated between sneezing and eating a variety of chips and other items with zero nutritional value.

Then on went the jetliner on a journey that had somehow ascended from long to what felt like never-ending.

It was evening when up toward the lavishly appointed Peninsula Hotel in Beijing came five weary travelers: Wesley and Jenny Phillips, Calvin, Carrie, and Beverly Steele.

As bellhops grabbed their luggage, they entered the lobby, where Jenny stopped her companions.

"To get onto Beijing time," she announced, "and in the hope of feeling human again, I'm inviting everyone to dinner in an hour."

"But –" said her husband, only to have Jenny cut him off with uncharacteristic firmness.

"No *buts*," she stated emphatically. Then, with a smile, Jenny turned to Calvin and Carrie.

"Okay?"

Too taken aback to resist, the two of them nodded.

Several minutes later, a bellhop led Calvin and Carrie into an opulent hotel room. There he turned on the lights, accepted a tip from Calvin, then left them alone.

"This is insane," Carrie stated immediately.

"You're telling me?"

"And no way in the world do I go to that dinner."

At the designated hour, seated with his wife at a large booth at the Peninsula's formal restaurant, Wesley Phillips was aghast to see Jenny, whose demeanor gave the impression that she had already consumed far more than appropriate, down another full flute of Dom Perignon.

"I think that's enough," Phillips stated.

"Says who?"

Jenny flamboyantly gestured to a waiter, who was in the process of refilling her glass when up toward the booth came Calvin with none other than Carrie.

"Mr and Mrs' son and girlfriend?" the waiter asked. "Very cute."

The only one to speak was Jenny, who ignored the question.

"Another bottle, please," she said.

"Know how much that costs here?" asked Phillips.

"And all the plane tickets were cheap?"

"Ready for menus?" asked the waiter.

"When the other person arrives," Jenny replied.

As the waiter bustled off, Jenny turned to Calvin and Carrie.

"You two thinking of getting married?" she asked.

When neither one of them offered even a peep, Jenny turned to her husband.

"Maybe you should be the best man, since you've been such a benefactor."

Up came the waiter with another bottle of Champagne, which he opened with a *Pop!*, then poured for all four of them.

Immediately, Jenny raised her flute to toast.

"To young love!" she exclaimed.

Uncomfortably, the others clinked glasses and took a sip, with the exception of Jenny, who drained hers in one gulp, then faced Carrie.

"Is he good in bed," Jenny asked, gesturing toward Calvin. "Forgive me for asking, but with Wesley here, it took him ages to get the hang of it."

"Jenny –" Wesley started to protest, only to be cut off.

"You know it's true," Jenny said before turning again to face Carrie. "But you don't need to know about that. Or about all the girls to whom he's made all sorts of promises over the years."

"What in hell are you babbling about?" Wesley Phillips demanded.

"Babbling, huh?" asked Jenny. "You think I don't know? But there's a difference between knowing and having my nose rubbed in it – with our very own house guest as the goddamn beard!"

With Calvin at a loss as to what to say or do, Carrie rose.

"Forgive me –" she mustered.

As she started toward the door, Calvin got to his feet.

But before Calvin could follow Carrie, Jenny grabbed his arm.

"Please wait!" she insisted.

Calvin stopped and faced Jenny, who pointed at her husband.

"Look at him," she ordered.

"Jenny, for God's sake!"

Paying no attention to Phillips, Jenny continued.

"Think seriously. Is this who – or what – you really want to be?"

Calvin studied Wesley Phillips with the closest he could come to a pair of brand new eyes, but said nothing. Instead, he lingered for a brief moment, then suddenly strode toward the exit, leaving Wesley Phillips no choice but to face his wife.

"What exactly do you want?" the CEO implored.

"The house, the kids, and every other goddamn thing to which I'm entitled!"

"Please, can't we talk this through?"

"Not anymore!"

In the hotel lobby, an elevator door opened and out stepped Beverly Steele, who immediately spotted Carrie, whose eyes were filled with tears.

"Whoa, girl! Whoa!" Beverly exclaimed before Carrie could step into the elevator.

"I'm sorry, I —"

With unexpected tenderness, Beverly put her arms around Carrie and held her until the sobbing diminished, then used her sleeve to dry Carrie's eyes.

Taking Carrie's hand, Beverly led her away from the hubbub of the lobby, just as out from the restaurant came Calvin.

Spotting the two women, Calvin followed at a distance, then observed quietly from afar as Beverly sat Carrie down in a quiet spot.

"Welcome to the wonderful world of Wesley Phillips," Beverly said softly.

"H-how do you know?"

"How do you think *I* wound up in LA? Thanks to his touching speech about feeling under-appreciated and suffocated in his marriage. Then one day I realized I wasn't the first, nor would I ever be the last."

"But you stayed."

"Instead of going back to mosquitoes the size of hummingbirds and a totally dead end life? I stayed and took the consolation prize: enough money and power to see me through bouts of bitterness and rage. But you're young. Why settle?"

With Calvin still observing, Carrie studied Beverly until a realization hit home.

"Talking like this —" she began.

"Yeah?"

"Can't it get you into trouble?"

"Don't worry about me, honey," Beverly assured her. "Yours truly is the one who knows where all the skeletons are buried. And let me tell you, there are lots and lots of skeletons!"

Not wanting to intrude, Calvin waited while the two

women finished talking, then watched as Carrie headed once again to the elevator.

Instead of following her, Calvin gave her a few minutes lead time by wandering around the hotel, and only then headed up to the room.

Carrie was frantically stashing her belongings in her suitcase when in stepped Calvin.

"Slow down," he said quietly. "We only have to be at the airport an hour before the flight."

"International means two hours," Carrie replied. "And besides, what's with this *we*?"

"If you're leaving, so am I."

"But —"

"*But*, nothing. And as for international, there's been a change in plans."

"What are you talking about?"

"Trust me, okay?" Calvin said. "It's all been arranged."

Not a word was said on the taxi ride to the airport, where Calvin took charge as they went through security.

Only when the two of them approached their designated boarding gate did Carrie realize what Calvin had chosen as their destination.

"Xi'an?" Carrie exclaimed.

"Unless you'd rather go to, say, Cleveland."

"But what about your job?"

"What job?"

It did not take long for Calvin's words to sink in.

"You're crazy!" Carrie said.

"Nope," replied Calvin. "In fact, for the first time in ages, I'm actually starting to feel sane."

On the flight to Xi'an, Calvin and Carrie were once again silent, but in a totally different way. With tension and acrimony dissolving, they felt comfortable with each other as never before.

For the first time ever, the two of them were one, accepting the world rather than either fighting it or hoping for something from it.

Brimming with anticipation, the two of them held hands as the plane prepared to land.

Stepping into the Xi'an airport after their flight, Carrie looked around in amazement.

"I can't believe we're actually here," she said.

"Truthfully," said Calvin, "neither can I."

Though heavy-duty sightseeing was no more a part of Calvin's DNA than wearing a tutu or singing karaoke, being in Xi'an – and especially with Carrie – made everything different. Together they merrily wore themselves out strolling through the narrow streets of the ancient walled city, filled with sesame oil factories and women cooking yummy persimmon cakes here, there, and everywhere. And seeing the justly celebrated vast underground fields of Terracotta Warriors. And wandering through the night market with its rows and rows of produce, clothes, and stands selling street food in every form imaginable.

For the first time since leaving New Jersey, Calvin was doing something neither based upon ambition, nor driven by an ulterior motive.

And for the first time since he became a *beard*, he was sharing a bed with a woman not dutifully, but freely, happily, joyfully.

And not just *any* woman, but with the one who for him stood above all others.

Though neither Calvin nor Carrie had the slightest clue as to what the future might hold, they were wonderfully, magically, miraculously together.

It was heaven on earth, which for Calvin translated into no doubts, no lists, no sleeplessness, and above all no more *Who am I?*

Week Eight

BASKETBALL IN HAND, out from the Gadzooks building stepped Alonzo Stevens the following Thursday at lunchtime.

As always, he started to dribble down the street, then stopped at the sound of a familiar voice.

"Got a sec?" asked Calvin, who was approaching.

"Rumor has it some crazy white dude just got himself hired to teach at Centennial High down in Compton," Alonzo said.

"Surprised?"

"Proud. Want to tell me about it?"

"Only if you'll accept my apology."

"For what?"

"Blowing you off the way I did."

"C'mon... So anyway, I'm listening —"

"How about we save it for dinner Saturday night?" asked Calvin.

"You, me, and Joy?"

"You, me, Joy, and Carrie."

"All right!" Alonzo exclaimed happily.

The two of them hugged, then started to walk in separate directions – Alonzo toward the park, Calvin toward the street.

But as the ex-intern headed toward the Honda Civic that was waiting near the curb, a beat-up Datsun pulled over toward him, then an innocent-looking youngish guy poked his head through the window.

"Any clue how I find 11201 Olympic?" the guy asked.

"Gadzooks?"

The Datson driver nodded proudly, then was surprised to see Calvin, who had just lived what felt like a lifetime in a mere matter of weeks, shrug as he pointed toward the monolith of a building behind him.

"Lots of luck," Calvin said.

Not knowing how to take Calvin's enigmatic statement, the

guy in the Datsun eyed him strangely.

Instead of lingering, Calvin strode toward the Honda Civic, where Carrie slid from behind the wheel into the passenger seat.

Opening the driver's side door, Calvin climbed in and faced Carrie.

"You're beautiful," he said.

"And hungry," she added.

"Which means –"

"Shut up and drive," they said in unison.

Sharing a laugh, the two of them kissed. Then Calvin turned on the ignition.

With no certainty about anything except that whatever life might bring them, they were ready to face together, off they went to start life anew.

More books from
Harvard Square Editions